BOUNDARY

THE BOOKS OF EVA

Also by Heather Terrell

Relic: The Books of Eva

HEATHER TERRELL
BOUNDARY

THE BOOKS OF EVA

Published in the United States by Soho Teen
an imprint of
Soho Press, Inc.
853 Broadway
New York, NY 10003

Library of Congress Cataloging-in-Publication Data

Terrell, Heather.
Boundary / Heather Terrell.
(The books of Eva ; [2])

ISBN 978-1-61695-620-2
eISBN 978-1-61695-198-6

1. Fantasy. I. Title.
PZ7.T274Bou 2014
[Fic]—dc23   2014027672

Interior illustrations © Ricardo Cortés
Interior design by Janine Agro, Soho Press, Inc.

Printed in the United States of America

10 9 8 7 6 5 4 3 2 1

For my three boys—Jim, Jack, and Ben

History of New North

"The Gods swept hurricanes across the world and warmed the polar ice caps—washing the Healing over mankind . . ."
—The Praebulum

"But before the seas covered nearly all of His lands, Father Earth listened to Mother Sun's pleas for mercy . . . He spared one last group of people—those of the Aerie." —The Lex

With guidance from the Gods, the Founders begin to write sacred texts, The Praebulum and The Lex, setting forth the rules by which the people of New North must live.

The Boundary lands launch a final raid against the Aerie. The New North's Gallants soundly defeat them.

As a reminder of New North's righteous supremacy, the Gods mandate taking the Boundary lands' people as servants for the Aerie.

1-4 A.H.
[After Healing]

Year Zero
[The Healing]

5-7 A.H.

8 A.H.

27 A.H.

68 A.H.

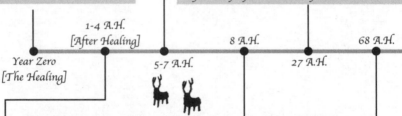

The Aerie Gate is finished. On the last day of construction, Founder Edmund discovers the first Relic: an altar to the false god Apple.

With guidance from the Gods, Edmund names himself First Archon and establishes the Testing and the Chronicles. Founder Mikhail, as witness, becomes First Lexor. Founder Sven, as Leading Gallant, becomes First Basilikon.

The Triad is now complete. The Founders finish The Praebulum and The Lex, thanks to the Gods.

The Founders begin to build the sacred enclave of the Aerie within the Ring, the great wall of New North.

Gallants repel attacks and banish those not chosen by the Gods to the barren ice-world beyond the Ring: the Boundary lands.

Construction of the Basilikon is completed. The first Feast Days are established.

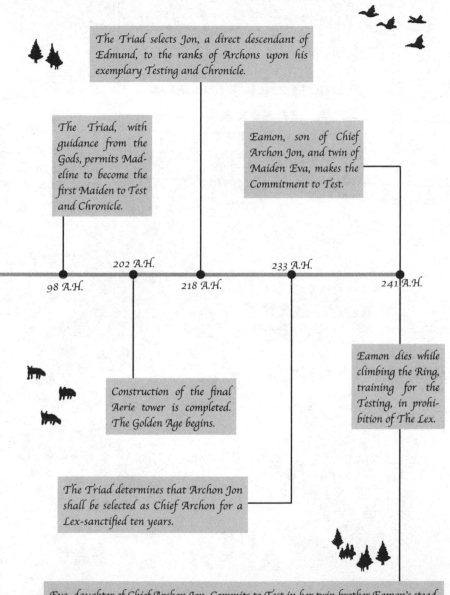

The Triad selects Jon, a direct descendant of Edmund, to the ranks of Archons upon his exemplary Testing and Chronicle.

The Triad, with guidance from the Gods, permits Madeline to become the first Maiden to Test and Chronicle.

Eamon, son of Chief Archon Jon, and twin of Maiden Eva, makes the Commitment to Test.

202 A.H.

233 A.H.

98 A.H.

218 A.H.

241 A.H.

Eamon dies while climbing the Ring, training for the Testing, in prohibition of The Lex.

Construction of the final Aerie tower is completed. The Golden Age begins.

The Triad determines that Archon Jon shall be selected as Chief Archon for a Lex-sanctified ten years.

Eva, daughter of Chief Archon Jon, Commits to Test in her twin brother Eamon's stead.

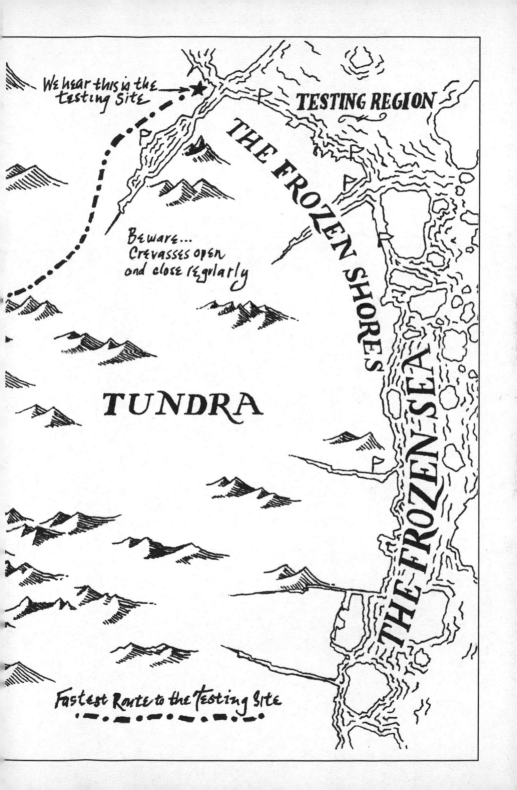

BOUNDARY

THE BOOKS OF EVA

PROLOGUE

Lukas stands on the highest point of the Ring. He knows the position is too exposed, too risky in daylight, but he has no choice. Not if he wants to see Eva. He strains for a glimpse through a small crack in the ice-roof of the Basilika. If he angles himself just right, he may catch something of the ceremony proceeding behind the colorful stained ice-windows. Perhaps the swoop of a Gallant's silvery cloak. Maybe even the trailing hem of Eva's white gown.

Bracing himself against the bitter wind, he walks up toward the edge and looks over the top of the snow cornice. In his eagerness, he moves too close. His misstep sends *qetrar* flying down the side of the Ring. The chunks of ice-crust crash into one another as they fall, making a noise that no Ring-Guard could ignore. Not even the laziest of them.

Ducking behind an ice-mound, Lukas slows his breath and stills his body. He leans into a depression, willing his inky sealskin coat and black hair to blend into its shadows. The *unalaq* picks up, and his coat flaps in its wind. He grabs the coat and pulls it close to his body. To the eyes of the Ring-Guards—poorly trained in the Boundary ways of seeing in ice and snow—he will look like nothing more than a shadow. Which is all he is to them, anyway.

The thud of clumsy footsteps grows louder. After thousands of *siniks* on the ice, the Aerie people should be more nimble, yet still they walk as heavily as bears, even on such an important day as this. But it's just another example of their dependence on the Boundary. The Aerie would starve if there was no one to hunt for them; they'd scare a deaf rabbit away.

The sound of the footsteps stops close to his hiding place.

Lukas slides his bow out of his pack and turns it toward the ground to notch his arrow. In one single, silent movement, he draws his bow and brings it up to his face. He holds it there as he listens to the Ring-Guards.

"Looks like the ice fell from here."

"The cornice seems weak. Probably just couldn't hold the ice-crust."

"So some pieces broke off and slid down on their own?"

"That's what I'm guessing."

"It's possible. Still, the Triad issued strict orders about today—"

"Come on. We still have the rest of the perimeter to patrol."

The voices trail off, and the footsteps fade. Lukas

exhales and lowers his bow, watching his breath form frozen clouds.

He dares to step out onto the Ring again and peers down onto the Aerie. The open spaces at the Ring's center—usually bustling—are empty. All the Aerie folk are within the Basilika's walls. A stark reminder that this ceremony is not for the Boundary. The Boundary are always *ellami*, outside. Unless they're serving at the Feast afterward.

Lukas waits, watching through his soldered-together metal tubes. Without warning, the sunlight intensifies. The bright rays afford him a view into the rift in the Basilika's roof. The view is limited, but it serves his purposes.

The procession of Gallants, Maidens, Lords, and Ladies begins the ceremonial walk down the Basilika's knave—it reminds him of the slow journey of an iceberg across the Frozen Sea. Cold and inhuman. Lukas can make out only their white and silver-grey finery, not their faces. He can barely hear their chanting. It's the purr of insects on a rare summer night. He's not certain how he'll identify Eva.

Anger courses through him, anger at himself. He alone is at fault for this. His acts brought Eva to this juncture. The guilt is his to shoulder; it doesn't matter that his acts were *ajurnama*, that they could not be helped. Their lies gave him no choice. He'd like nothing more than to send one of his arrows down into the icy parade to stop her ceremony with that tedious Gallant. But he must only bear witness.

At that moment he sees it. A flash of her long auburn hair cascading down the back of her white gown. Eva. *His* Eva.

No, she is more. She does not belong to him alone. She is the *Angakkuq*. The one who will spark the *true* Healing, the one who will melt the frozen sea of lies and destroy this place forever.

I.

Junius 20
Year 242, A.H.

I stand at the back of the Basilika, waiting. I watch as every friend I've ever had, every highborn Aerie I've ever known, promenades down the nave first, a resplendent sea of white and silver. The men's elaborate cloaks of animal hides are bleached white from Mother Sun; the women's sumptuous gowns of undyed fabrics, scrubbed with ivory, are embroidered with rare silver thread that shine as if just made.

These robes may only be worn on this particular occasion, the Betrothal ceremony.

Except for a Union day when a Maiden and her Gallant alone wear blue, a Betrothal is the only time The Lex permits the entire Aerie to deviate from our usual somber blacks and browns. Only then does The Lex allow us to focus on the future—Unions and children—rather than remind us of our terrible past. On this special day, we Aerie band together in a swath of the purest snow as a plea to the Gods to give mankind another chance.

The rays of Her Sun pour through ice-windows colored in the symbols of the Father, the Mother, and the Healing. The day is unseasonably warm, even for spring. The warmth makes the walls weep, as if the Sun Herself is crying colored tears.

Here I am at the center of it all, some kind of offering to the Gods. The trussed-up milky-white emblem of mankind's hope for a second chance. But I am a fraud.

I draw a Maidenly smile upon my face for the Aerie people to see—I know they're all watching—but really I feel like crying along with Her. Not because my Betrothed is Jasper. He is the best kind of Gallant, and I believe he's in love with me. I'm lucky in this, because love isn't a prerequisite for Unions. In fact, it's a rarity, and I almost feel guilty that Jasper feels so strongly for me. After all, our Betrothal is born from a ruse.

No, the reason I feel like sobbing is that I mourn the loss of my old self. I used to be a guileless child playing with my twin Eamon before he fell from the Ring. I was a trusting Maiden in search of Testing glory in her dead brother's name. I stood within these sacred walls and worshipped the Gods with my whole spirit.

No more. One night with Lukas in the Boundary lands melted that innocence.

A shift in the music awakens me from my dark thoughts. The deep chanting of the Basilikons becomes more layered, more intense. Their polyphonic pleas for the Gods to bless this Union—voices only, no instruments in the

Basilika—escalate. I look over at the Chief Basilikon, who nods in my direction.

This is my signal.

I muster my courage, gather the folds of my white gown heavy with embroidery and beadwork, and take the first step down the long nave. Silver and gold orbs—symbols of Father Earth and Mother Sun—stare down at me from the chancel. I suddenly feel that the Gods Themselves see through my artifice. A shiver passes through me at the thought of Their judgment.

Then the doubt creeps in. The fear vanishes, and in its wake is something I cannot name. This new feeling I have, it feels like a sickness. Do the Gods even exist? I believed in the Father and Mother for so long, but now I wonder.

As I continue my procession down the nave, I see the smiles of my friends and neighbors, even some Aerie I don't really know. Hundreds of faces, maybe even a thousand, beaming at me. I am the cornerstone of their hopes. I am about to become a newly Betrothed Maiden, and I'm already their newest Archon. I am something special and new, and therefore a gift from the Gods.

Without slowing my progress, I bestow my own small smile upon that sea of faces, always careful to keep my gaze downcast in Maidenly modesty. In truth, I dare not look any one of them in the eyes. I fear that my eyes will reveal my true purpose, the whole reason I continue with this subterfuge. Because only I know my true mission: I must uncover who among them killed my brother.

II.

Junius 24
Year 242, A.H.

One by one, the tight stays of my gown loosen. As my Companion Katja slowly undoes the bindings of my corset, I sigh in relief. I've been laced up in my somber Basilika gown since the first bell of morning—suffering through the last in an endless number of services blessing me as Archon. At long last I can breathe.

The heather-grey gown drops to the floor, and I reach for my black sealskin Archon uniform. The tunic, pants, and cloak look almost exactly as they did during the Testing—except they're now a whole lot cleaner, and they've been embroidered with the Triad symbol.

I finger the red stitching; it looks like my mother's fine handiwork. She got the Archon for which she's longed. Just not the one she expected.

What would this day have held if Eamon hadn't died? Would I be helping him prepare for his first day of Archon training? Would I be betrothed to Jasper and ready to enter a life like my mother's? Even though I've never wanted to be anything like my mother, I'd choose that path if it would bring my brother back.

Seeing me pause, Katja hurries to my side. Shaking out the uniform, she holds out the pants so that I can step into them. I take them back from her instead. "It's all right, Katja. I can manage this on my own."

"Oh, no, Lady Margret would never forgive me."

"Are you Lady Margret's Companion or mine, Katja?"

Her body stiffens. "Yours—"

"If you don't tell Lady Margret that I got dressed on my own, then I won't, either," I interrupt. My tone is stern, but I am smiling.

Katja hesitates. My request is certainly outside the bounds of The Lex; secrets are never, ever permitted. But I am an Archon now, and my rule is law, too.

Nodding, she starts to curtsy and says, "Good day, Maid—" Then she stops herself. She isn't quite sure how to address me. No one is.

She tries again. "Good day . . . Archon."

I force a laugh. I need to lighten this exchange. "Just call me Eva. It's a lot easier."

Backing out of the room, head down, she mutters, "I couldn't do that."

She's right, of course, and I've only made her more uncomfortable. Such familiarity between Boundary and Aerie people is forbidden by The Lex. Katja would be disciplined by Boundary and Aerie alike if someone overheard her. Never mind that Lukas and I more than bridged that gap.

Careful not to call me anything at all, Katja closes the door behind her.

Alone for a few ticks, I kneel on the floor next to my bed. I slide my hand under a loose floorboard and force my fingers into the crevice below, until I feel my treasure: Elizabet's amulet. Lukas taught me the real name for the pendant—a "flash drive"—but I will always think of it as an amulet, because Elizabet wore it around her neck the night she died. She'd put her hopes and dreams into it, and by doing so, she made it magic.

I slip the amulet around my neck. No matter the risk, I want Elizabet with me on my first day as Archon. She's the one who got me to this place, after all. Well, Elizabet and Eamon.

Pulling the black tunic over my head, I arrange the neckline to cover my secret possession. Then I pull on the seal-skin pants and cloak. They feel so light and comfortable after all the long *siniks* in gowns. I remember how peculiar the uniform felt when I first wore it for the Testing. Now I prefer it.

Just this once, I wish I had a mirror to see my reflection. I feel so different than when I set out on this path. I'm certain my face must show it. But once more, I must guess at how I look—ever since I returned the only proper mirror in the Aerie to my father after the Testing. It's telling that Father chose not to return it to the mantel in our home but instead locked it in his private treasury. His precious Relic ultimately won him the Sacred Role of Chief Archon. But though we've never discussed it, Father and I both know it served me well during my own Testing, thanks to Lukas. Lukas insisted I take it, knowing it could be a tool and not just a Testament to Vanity. In violation of everything we believe, Father agreed. He knew it could save my life. I wonder how much else he knows about the wisdom of the Boundary.

I take a deep breath at the top of the stairs. My parents will be waiting at the bottom, eager to send me off with blessings for my first day of training at the Hall of Archons. I stride down the steps with a confidence I don't really feel and am surprised to find that Jasper is waiting, too.

"Your Betrothed wanted to say his farewells," my mother announces on Jasper's behalf, as if *he* concocted this meeting. Of course she arranged this. Any chance she gets to tether me to my role as Betrothed instead of Archon, she takes.

I glance over at Jasper, so handsomely Gallant and Nordic blond. He gives me a small, knowing smile—he understands my mother almost as well as I do—and takes my hand in his. Now that we are Betrothed, we are permitted to touch in this limited way.

"I'm glad that you came," I say. Truly I am. After playing at so many ill-fitting roles these past weeks, it's a relief to be with someone who understands something of the truth. He alone knows how our Betrothal really happened, forged under the shining light of the Ring-Guards' threats instead of during an impassioned moment on the turret, as we told our parents. Our parents believed us, or pretended to, anyway. For them, it was relief or delight or both. And we felt it, too. After that, Jasper and I embarked on a whirlwind of Feasts and Basilika services, culminating in the Betrothal ceremony, which was so lavish that in comparison, the actual Union festivities may feel anticlimactic.

I squeeze his hand. Jasper's presence brings me comfort today. He also understands that no matter how hard

I fought for the Archon Laurels in the Testing in Eamon's name, I have mixed feelings. But he thinks my discomfiture stems from grief over my brother; he knows nothing about the fear I feel as the so-called *Angakkuq*. How could I tell him about the Boundary people's belief in my sacred role without revealing too much? I can barely admit to myself that their belief is real, or what it could possibly mean.

My mind flashes back to that strange night—my secret trip to the Boundary lands, to Lukas's grandmother. What she said still sounds crazy: that I am the *Angakkuq*, a shaman mediator between the Earth and the spirit world. And that the Boundary has been waiting for me, the seeker of the truth, for over a generation. Normally I don't disagree with Elders—The Lex is very clear on the subject of respect—but while I accept the duty to unearth the truth and change things if I must, I have to refuse the *Angakkuq* title.

If the Aerie's religious beliefs are false, as I'm starting to believe, then doesn't that mean the Boundary's belief could be false, too? Again, I think of my father's mirror. He believes something of what they believe, even though he could never admit it. What other secrets is he keeping?

Still, even if I don't buy into this *Angakkuq* notion, it doesn't mean that the Boundary will give up on the idea. They are relying on me even if their motives are based on some wild dream. I feel their expectations on my shoulders as well as my own.

"May the Gods travel with you," Jasper says.

His words surprise me at first; they constitute the ritual blessing for those few permitted to journey beyond the Ring. I'm just heading to the Hall of Archons. I realize, however, that his words are fitting. This is the start of a pilgrimage, and it may well take me outside the comfort and safety of the Aerie.

"May the Gods travel with you also," I answer.

His own journey begins today, too. He'll start training for the Forge, the competition for the position of Lexor. If he wins, he'll join one of the three ruling groups in the Triad, the one charged with enforcing The Lex. It occurs to me, not for the first time, that our Union will be a powerful one.

We stand together for a long tick.

My father clears his throat. "Eva, we must go. Your fellow Archons will be awaiting you. And me."

My mother chimes in. "Your brother would not have been late on his first day as Archon."

She certainly knows how to reach me. At the mention of Eamon, I try to release Jasper's hand, but his fingers are still wrapped around mine. He doesn't want to let go. "Be careful, Eva," he whispers.

I smile at him in reassurance. "You'll probably see me later this week," I whisper back. There are no guarantees, however. I could spend months training in the Hall of Archons by day and dining at home by night, or I could be sent on a Frozen Shore dig by the Midday Bell.

"Eva," my father says again. This time, his voice brooks no delay.

Jasper releases me. My father and I move toward the door. I glance back, and the unprecedented nature of this moment hits me. This is the first time in Aerie history that a Maiden leaves her Gallant at home as she heads off to her calling.

III.

Junius 24
Year 242, A.H.

My father and I step out into the busy world of the Aerie. Even though the Prime Bell has not yet started to ring, the streets are hurried and crowded. Boundary stewards from the Grain Keep rush past us, delivering steaming loaves of bread to Triad homes. Maidens and Ladies line up outside the Basilika for a special sermon on their sacred role in New North. But there is one constant among all the people, Aerie and Boundary: When they see us, they pause and bow. A sighting of the Chief Archon and his daughter, Eva, will provide the people with excellent gossip for their evening meals. The first female Archon in history, on her very first day of Archon service!

I feel a new kind of pride in spite of my misgivings. I've

always felt proud walking at my father's side or standing alongside him during ceremonies, but this is different. The respect accorded by the people we pass isn't for him alone. It's for me, too.

But then almost instantly, everything feels wrong. This should be Eamon's moment. No matter how hard I worked to win the Laurels in his memory, Eamon will never have a chance to live his dreams, whatever they might have been. He was cheated out of his life. How dare I try to fulfill his destiny for him?

I push away my dark thoughts and work hard to match my father's stride through the warren of narrow streets. Our sealskin coats trail behind us like ravens' wings, and we are moving so fast I almost feel like we are flying, almost like I felt coursing over the snow on my sled during the Testing. Maidens must always move with careful grace—*Let no inelegance overtake your movements; instead keep the slow passage of Her Sun ever in your mind*—so this is new to me. But now I'm an Archon. It's kind of liberating. I try to focus on that.

My father doesn't mention it, but I know my long moment with Jasper is the reason we must hurry. We have to make it through the front doors of the Hall of Archons before the Prime Bell sounds its final sixth chime. Otherwise, the Archon-Guards will lock it for the day. It would not only embarrass me, but my father as well. There are Aerie who would enjoy seeing that happen—my own mother among them, if only to remind me of my true role as a Maiden.

Just as I spy the ice-spires of the Hall of Archons over the top of the Raiments Keep, the first bell of Prime sounds. My father grabs my hand. Panic must show on my face, because he smiles. "We can't have you late on your first day, can we?"

"We won't be late."

Hand in hand, we sprint down the final street before we reach the small plaza in front of the Hall of Archons. The usually stone-faced Archon-Guards look shocked to see their stoic leader breathless and ruddy. I empathize. This day is indeed unlike any other. I wonder if they think of the sacrifices that have been made—chief among them Eamon's life—so that I can enter this sacred place. As the Ring-Guards heave open the thick metal doors, I compose myself.

It is dark inside, save for the torchlight. No cheery welcome awaits. Only a fearsome line of black-uniformed, expressionless Archons are assembled, facing me from the back of the Hall. The doors screech and clang shut behind us. Many of these men are familiar. I've Feasted with them, prayed to the Gods alongside them, and played with their children, but their faces bear no hint of recognition or Gallantry. I glance over at my father. No evidence of his kindly reassurance remains, either. The hand that helped me along a few ticks ago has passed me off to his underlings. I am no longer Eva—daughter, Maiden, fellow Founding family member, Betrothed, Schoolchild. I am simply the newest Archon.

During the long days before the Testing and the even longer *siniks* of the Testing itself, I had envisioned so much about becoming an Archon. But I didn't envision this day. I wonder if the Testing is such an ordeal to mask what is truly terrifying: Archon service itself.

I manage to harden my own face and nod when one of the more senior Archons directs me to the back of the line.

As I march past the dark, watchful eyes of the other Gallants, I remind myself that I won the Laurels as they did. I deserve to be here, too.

I must be strong. If I allow even a tiny chink in my armor, the others will see my true purpose. So I make my way to the back of the queue, where I am the youngest and the shortest without question, and repeat to myself, "You are just an Archon here to do your sacred duty." Nothing more, nothing less. I don't allow myself to think of my real purpose, of uncovering the truth about New North and along with it, the murderer of my brother.

My father starts a prayer, and we join our voices with his. "Oh, Father and Mother, who art in the Heavens, Hallowed be Thy names. Thy Kingdom has come, Thy wills have been done . . ." I try to lose myself in the chant I've uttered so many times, the sacred reminder that the Aerie is the fulfillment of the Gods' prophecy, that we are Their endgame. And that as Archons, we are here to keep mankind in that endgame.

My eyes drift as my lips form the familiar words. The walls and ceiling of the Hall are covered in the symbol of the Triad. It's one way of reminding us of who holds the control, I guess. A few windows dot the thick ice walls lined with shelves, arrayed with Relics from past Testings. Mounted on one shelf are a grouping of artifacts—bowls, boxes with small handles in many colors, metal cans, and bags imprinted with crude words and drawings.

Are these the sorts of artifacts Lukas would want me to investigate? I don't think I've ever heard them mentioned in the Chronicles of past Testors, but then, the Archons often undertake excavations about which the people of New North hear nothing.

I hear my name. Reluctantly, I shift my gaze from the Relics to my father.

"The Lex mandates that each Neophyte Archon be assigned a Mentor Archon who can train the newly Laureled member of the Triad. This selection is undertaken with great care by the senior Archons. This relationship is key to the Neophyte's understanding of the Gods' will. For our newest Archon Eva, we have chosen Archon Laurence as Mentor."

IV.

Junius 24
Year 242, A.H.

A rchon Laurence?

At first I think there's been a mistake. Laurence is the second-in-charge under my father, far too busy to serve as Mentor. Usually a seasoned but relatively junior Archon would be chosen for this role.

Maybe I should view the selection as a compliment, but I'm worried that the others will see it as favoritism. Or maybe I should see it as my father overprotecting me, as a female in a male's world? Then there's the fact that Laurence expects the Chief position when my father steps down from his ten-year term. He can't be thrilled about this appointment, either. Not only am I the first Maiden Archon, I'm possible competition: The Chief is selected solely on the strength of his or her Chronicle, not his years of service. And everyone keeps talking about how much the people loved my Chronicle.

My father finishes his speech, and the Archons disperse. No one tells me where to go. Only my father and Laurence remain, engaged in deep conversation. For an endless tick, I'm standing in my queue spot in the Hall, awkwardly awaiting their command.

"Archon Eva," my father calls.

Walking over to his side, I answer, "Yes, Chief." Calling my father "Chief" feels artificial, like we are playing a Schoolchild game. But it must be done.

"You know Archon Laurence, of course." My father gestures to him.

Out of long habit, I start to curtsy. Stopping myself, I bow to my senior as would any other Archon, and wait for Laurence to speak. He doesn't. He merely lowers his grey eyes and silvery-blond head. It's not quite a bow in return. It's an insult. Such deviance from polite rituals of greeting—whether Archon or Maiden—is defiance itself.

Glaring at Laurence, my father says, "I'm certain that Archon Laurence will serve as a dutiful Mentor to you, Eva. The Lex says that Triad members must obey the authority of their leaders above all else. Isn't that right, Archon Laurence?"

Laurence waits a long tick before answering. "The Lex does indeed say that, Chief."

My father's voice hardens, matching the flicker of anger across his face. "As an obedient member of the Triad, you will comply with The Lex and conform to the authority of your leaders in the matter of Archon Eva, correct?" It is not a question, but a command.

"Of course, my Chief." Laurence answers with a deep

bow that hides his steely eyes. I'm certain they would not display the same submission that his words suggest.

Father always says to keep your enemies close. For a split tick, I wonder whether Laurence is the killer that I've been seeking. His loathing of me and Father is ill-conceived. No, he seems too self-protective and much too self-serving to take such risks, even if he viewed Eamon as a threat, which I'm guessing he did.

"As I thought," my father answers, his voice lighter. "You and Archon Eva may be dismissed to begin her instruction."

Laurence and I bow to my father.

I really must start thinking of him as Chief in the Hall of Archons. I turn and retreat to the vestibule at the end of the Hall.

When Laurence stops walking, I do as well.

Another Archon stands there. At first I don't recognize him in the darkness of the windowless space, especially after the relative brightness of the Hall. After my eyes adjust, I realize that I know him from Feast days.

It's Archon Theo. He won his Testing year nearly forty years ago, making him the oldest Archon still serving.

Why is he here?

Laurence finally deigns to speak to me. "Archon Eva?" he grunts. "I will see you in two weeks, at which time we will leave for an excavation on the Frozen Shores. Until then, Archon Theo will train you."

Even in the shadows, I detect a sneer—a sneer that Laurence surely wanted me to see.

Before I can ask any questions, he slips off into one of the many hallways that extend from this spot like a squid's tentacles. So this is how Laurence follows the authority of his leader. He's palming off his mentoring responsibilities to a frail old man.

My father would be furious. Should I tell him? If I do, there is no doubt he will inflict his fury on Laurence, and Laurence will know why. So Laurence is testing me. He wants to prove that I'm just another Maiden who will run whining to her family.

No, I'll wait for my father to find out through other means, as he certainly will. Besides, his anger wouldn't really be about the mistreatment of his daughter. But everyone else would see it that way. I don't want to draw any more attention to myself—more attention than serving as the only female Archon in history draws all by itself.

I need to stay quiet if I'm to do my true work. I don't know what that work will entail, so I'm not willing to name it just yet—not even to myself. Quiet is what I shall become. A quiet little mouse scurrying in and out of the Hall's secret places.

V.

Junius 24
Year 242, A.H.

"You can't be happy about this reassignment of your education, Archon Eva," Archon Theo says as he leads me away. "I know how archaic I seem to a young Archon."

Is he baiting me? I think about how Eamon would respond, and I say, "I follow the authority and commands of my superiors. Happy doesn't factor into my thoughts, Archon Theo." I'm thankful that I'm walking behind the wizened old man; it allows me to keep my eyes hidden while I utter a complete untruth.

"The perfect response. Very nice, Archon Eva. Such stoicism and obedience will serve you well in this Hall." He turns around abruptly. His rheumy eyes look me up and down. "Just like your father."

Turning back around, he signals me to follow him down a sharp turn off the corridor. He walks quickly for a man of his years and girth, maybe trying to prove that he's still vital. "The Lex does not permit diagrams of the Hall of Archons. We must protect our Relics and our study of them by every means. You must rely on your internal sense of direction and your memory to guide you through our labyrinthine hallways." He chuckles. "But I'm guessing that if you won the Laurels, you've got a pretty well-developed sense of direction."

"Yes, Archon Theo."

"Good. You'll need it in this maze. You will have much to learn in a short time, and you can't waste a tick by getting lost. Understood?"

"Understood, Archon Theo."

The passage narrows, its ice walls more rough-hewn. He points out a bright room, full of long tables strewn with objects. My heart quickens: the Conservation Chamber. Two unfamiliar Archons hover over the strange artifacts, examining them with a tool I've never seen before. It is black and C-shaped with a tube at the top. The Archons slide bits and pieces under the tube, then peer down the other end. The tool looks like a Relic itself, as if it should be studied rather than doing the studying. But Theo's pace is fast, and I don't have the chance to linger and watch them work.

Just as I commit that chamber to memory, Theo points out others. We twist down endless hallways, turning in one direction or another at what appear to be random forks—passing the Receiving Chamber, the Chamber of Equipment, the Examination Chamber, the Chamber of Records, the Map Chamber, and on and on. All places I've heard my father mention over the years, but of which I had no clear sense. Now his world is becoming mine.

I also notice that the connecting corridors are cut with at least one arched hole in the ice walls, like ice-windows without the ice-glass. All open onto an interior courtyard. Their placement helps me organize the layout of the Hall of Archons in my mind.

There's a roar from the courtyard, and I strain for a glimpse.

Theo pauses as well. "That's the Yard. It's used for the teaching of advanced ice climbing and excavation techniques. You will have the chance to train there later this afternoon, after the Midday Bell."

I nod, and he hurries toward the only staircase I've seen so far. Two guards carrying bows and arrows, knives, and other weaponry stand at the base of the stairs. No other place in the Hall or its corridors is similarly protected.

Theo stops. Waving grandly, he says, "The Offices of the Chief and the Vault of Archons are located up there."

I nod, but I'm suspicious. Why are we making a special stop here?

"Most Archons—especially our most junior—have no need to mount these stairs. The Offices of the Chief are not the place for them, nor is the Vault of Archons. But you must mark this place in your internal map, as you will be making use of the Vault, where past records of excavations are stored."

I nod, my heart thumping. This is the exact sort of place Lukas told me to locate. But I hadn't dreamed that I'd find it on my first day, or that I'd be granted access to it. Trying not to sound overly curious, I ask, "What sort of work would you like me to perform in the Vault?"

He smiles a little. "Ah, I hear the disappointment in your voice, Archon Eva. You'd rather train in the Yard than spend your ticks poring over dusty archives?"

"No, Archon Theo. I didn't mean—"

"You don't have to apologize. I know the Yard is where most young Archons want to be."

I can't help but think of Eamon's long bells in the Library, researching past Testings for his own preparations—of all the wealth of information it yielded him and me. "I thought the records of past excavations were kept in the Library."

"Some Testing documents are indeed collected there. Other Testing records are kept in the Vault, as well as the Archons' own private excavations."

"Of course." I fall silent. *Careful,* I tell myself. I must keep my excitement, my interest, guarded.

He pauses. "Don't you wonder what you'll be doing up there in the Vault?"

I almost smile, but I'm frightened. "Yes, Archon Theo."

"The Site to which you'll be traveling with Archon Laurence has been excavated once before. Many years ago. But then the ice shifted, and for the safety of the Archons, the Site was closed. Only now have the Gods decided to open the crevasse once more. So you will be researching that earlier excavation. The research will likely be dull. But we must make certain that we don't retread the ground of those earlier Archons. Or miss any areas they deemed promising."

I nod again, hoping my face is as impassive as my voice. "I'm honored to be doing such important work, Archon Theo."

"When you're coughing on the dust and ice particles of the past, you won't feel so honored," he replies.

I wonder why he's trying to make me feel bad about this assignment. Is this his subtle way of telling me what he really thinks about a Maiden as Archon? Or is some other message at work? Is he trying to tell me what he really thinks of Laurence and that he's on my side? I can't guess, and it really doesn't matter. All that matters is that I'm going to be granted access to the Vault.

"When was the Site last excavated? The one to which I'll be traveling?" I ask.

"In Year 98, after the Healing, It was a Testing excavation," he says as he leads me up the stairs.

Interesting, I think, and for all kinds of reasons. I know that Testing year. It was the year that one of only two other females besides me Tested. It was the year of Madeline.

VI.

Junius 24
Year 242, A.H.

I excuse myself before the Attendants serve the final course of sweets—dried figs, cheese, and honey cakes, which used to be my favorite. But I haven't craved sweets since the Testing; they taste too cloying, too intense. Even though my parents and Jasper offer their understanding when I say I am exhausted, I know they are disappointed. They hunger for details about my first day as Archon. I am in no mood to share, nor do I have to—everyone here knows that much of what goes on inside the Hall belong to Archons alone.

Mostly, though, I want to avoid any mention of Archon Laurence's abandonment of me to Archon Theo. I can't stand another tick of the contrivance.

My parents stand by the arched doorway to the dining

hall as Jasper and I part, chaperones as The Lex commands. Only after our Union can we be alone.

"I'm just happy that you'll be in the Aerie for at least two more weeks," Jasper whispers as he bows and kisses my outstretched hand.

"Me, too," I whisper back.

"Our Union cannot happen soon enough," he says and looks into my eyes. I see such longing in them that I blush.

He releases my hand. As the Attendant pulls open the weighty wooden door, Jasper turns back and waves. I raise my hand in farewell. A mixture of sadness and guilt rises within me, and I lower my eyes.

The stairs feel as though they've multiplied since I walked up them this morning after the Basilika services. As I drag my feet up step by step, I tell myself that I'm simply tired from the early rising and the long day. That it isn't the heaviness of my secret burden weighing me down. That I can handle it.

I reach the last stair and hear my father mutter, "It was hard, Margret, seeing her in the Hall."

"I'm sure it was, Jon," my mother answers, her voice a Lady-whisper. "To see your daughter among all those male faces." I can almost picture her leaning across the wide Feasting table to touch my father's hand in a gentle show of reassurance and solidarity. My mother's defining feature is her fierce, unwavering loyalty to our family. Her vision of our family, that is. But she has a genuine and Lady-like love of my father, I think. That is her saving grace.

"That is not the reason, Margret."

"No?"

"No." He makes a sound sort of like choking. "I kept

looking at Eva's face and seeing Eamon there instead. I
know he's gone, but I've imagined his face in the Hall for
so many years—"

His voice breaks off, and I freeze. He's crying. I've only
ever heard my father cry once before, the day the Ring-
Guards brought my brother's body home.

Katja sees me frozen on the top stair. She rushes to my
side. "Come—" She pauses, still unsure what to call me, but
wanting to please. "Eva, you are exhausted. Let me draw a
bath for you."

"No, Katja. I'll be fine." I wave off her efforts and enter
my bedroom alone. After shutting the door behind me, I
lean against it and slide down to sit my haunches, sobbing.

I'm not the only one playacting. My poor father—seemingly the essence of excitement and support today—is suffering along with me. The loss of Eamon haunts us all. I
try to calm down, to steady my breathing. I must put aside
my own worries about straddling two worlds—Maiden and
Testor, Betrothed and Archon, and most of all . . . whatever
the Aerie thinks I am and whatever I am truly to become.
This daily role-shifting must become instinctive and hidden.

I remind myself that in the end, there is only one purpose above all: to uncover the truth of Eamon's death. Perhaps the truth about New North is another knot that may
be untangled at the same time. But for now, I must com-
partmentalize.

It's not going to be as simple as I'd hoped to be that
quiet little mouse.

VII.

Junius 24
Year 242, A.H.

The tears will not stop. I try to stifle the sobs—I don't want my poor parents to hear me—but I feel like I can't breathe unless I let them out. All the grief that I've kept trapped inside me since Eamon died pours out in convulsive gasps. For months now, I've stuffed my sorrow into the darkest reaches of my spirit, thinking only of winning the Archon Laurels in his name, but finally, I must acknowledge the victory is empty. It will never bring my dead brother back to life.

As if watching someone else, I sink to my knees. Not in front of the diptych where I used to pray to the Gods, but right in the middle of my bedroom. I'm not sure to whom I'm praying anymore—what Gods exist, if any. But I must try.

"Whatever you are, whoever you are, please help me," I beg in a whisper.

The praying just makes me cry harder. The enormity and futility of what's ahead threatens to overwhelm me, and my chest heaves. Why did I ever think I could do this? I crumple, my head resting upon my knees. I feel a hand on my shoulder. I guess that no matter how hard I tried to keep quiet, Katja heard my sobs. Or worse, my parents.

I look up to see near-black eyes staring into mine. It's Lukas.

Even enveloped by sadness, I am still afraid—for the both of us, if anyone catches him here. In his eyes, I see that he understands; he's straddling two worlds, too. The Aerie where he serves those who believe Tech is evil—and his real home of the Boundary where his people know that Tech is only as evil as the hand that wields it. Lukas has been wrestling with these two worlds for a long time, probably his whole life.

He wipes a tear from my cheek. His gentle gesture make me cry harder; he was never one for softness. He wraps his arms around me, and whatever stones were left in my interior wall crumble. Yet the tears stop flowing. For the briefest of ticks, I feel safe.

"I've missed you, Eva," he says into the top of my head.

"And I you," I murmur into his shoulder. I wonder if we'd make these confessions if we were looking each other in the eye. Our relationship was built more on action than professed emotion.

"I wanted t-to see you—" he stammers, "to make sure you were okay."

"All this pretending . . ." I feel the tears coming again,

so I take a deep breath. I'm afraid to say more, as if words might unlock the tears.

"I know this is hard. Your training has started."

Did I imagine the understanding in his eyes? "It's not just becoming an Archon that's tough, Lukas."

"Of course not, Eva. So much is being asked of you. As *Angakkuq*."

I laugh a little. In the midst of all this grief and helplessness, the thought of me as some sort of shaman leader strikes me as funny. Or maybe just absurd. "I'm no *Angakkuq*."

"Yes, you are." His voice is firm.

He needs to understand. I pull back a little, but we are still seated, sort of tangled up in each other. "No, Lukas. I'm just a Maiden searching for answers—about my brother and about New North."

"The answers you seek are the exact ones the *Angakkuq* needs, too." He is insistent. "Eva the Maiden and Eva the *Angakkuq* are one and the same."

"No, they're not. Anyway, what does it matter if I'm the *Angakkuq* if we are both searching for the same things? Now that I'm an Archon—an insider like you wanted— I can find out the information we need. Whether I'm an Archon or Maiden or *Angakkuq* . . . it seems like semantics." I shrug.

"Semantics?"

Although he's not yelling, I can hear the anger in Lukas's voice. I pull farther back from him. "Yes." I stay resolute.

"It matters, Eva. So much has been sacrificed so that you can lead New North to the truth."

I recoil a little at the word. "Sacrifice? What do you mean by sacrifice?"

He sees my reaction and sighs. "*Sacrifice* is too strong. I mean we've been suffering in our ignorance for too long. And you alone in all of New North's history are unique. You alone can lead us from the darkness of past lies into the light of honesty."

I shake my head. "Listen to me, Lukas. I just want to find Eamon's killer and have him punished. And if that means I have to learn some unpleasant truths about New North in the process—truths that maybe got him killed— then so be it."

His eyes grow darker, sadder. "I wish you could understand how important you are, Eva."

I see myself reflected in his inky eyes, and I realize something. No matter how close I feel to Jasper these days, the only one who really knows me is Lukas. How can I have real feelings for Jasper when he only knows the public me? True, he knows more than most, but still only knows the construct I fashion—whether it's Maiden or Archon— whenever I face the world. Only with Lukas do I not wear any costume or mask or assume any role. I act the same way with him that I acted with Eamon. Although I feel very differently about Lukas than I felt about my brother.

Lukas runs his fingers along my cheek. Now that it's free of tears, I feel the roughness of his skin. I hold his hand and glance at it, if only to avoid staring into those stubborn, demanding black eyes. His hand is coarse and dry and heavily scarred. But very, very warm. I clasp it tightly.

"When will I see you next?" I ask.

"I'll come to you when I can."

"Are you still in the Boundary?"

"For now. I'm sure my next Aerie placement will come in soon." His voice is heavy; he sounds older than his years. I realize that I have no idea how old Lukas is. I always assumed he was the same age as me because he was Eamon's Companion. Even though he knows me better than anyone else, there's so much about him that I don't know. Questions I never asked.

"I'll try to wait," I tell him.

"No. You *must* wait for me to come to you. You don't realize how many eyes are upon you. We must keep you safe."

He releases my hand, and without glancing back, climbs out the window and into the night.

VIII.

Junius 25
Year 242, A.H.

"Again, Archon Eva," the masked Archon calls out. He wants me to scale the hundred-foot ice wall that dominates the Yard. This will be my sixth attempt. "Yes—" I stop.

It feels wrong and disrespectful not to address him by his Lex-given title, but I don't know what to call him. He didn't bother to introduce himself, and since I can't see his face underneath his sealskin mask, I don't know who he is. The mask is an oddity. The Aerie people are well-accustomed to the cold—we know nothing else—and generally only wear such masks in the dead of winter. In blizzards. Not on relatively warm spring days such as this.

I stare up at the man-made sheet of ice, which doubles as a cliff and a crevasse for training purposes. In my preparations for the Testing, Lukas had me scale much higher walls. During the Testing itself, I descended down a slick crevasse that had no bottom I could discern. I grew comfortable in even the most dangerous climbing conditions. Yet this artificial peak is defeating me. I can almost hear Lukas chuckling at my efforts, pushing me along with his taunts. His visit last night seems like a dream compared to the many vivid memories I have of our days training together.

It isn't the outcroppings or the soft patches or the hidden trenches—all carefully crafted by the Archons to hone our skills. Oh, no, I can handle those. It's the things on my feet, what the masked Archon calls "mountaineering boots."

For some reason he insists that we climb this faux glacier in this bizarre footgear instead of the bear claws which every Gallant—and one Maiden—knows how to use. Instead of claws for gripping, they have hard metal tips that slide off the ice. Instead of the insulated hide that molds to your foot and ankle, they are made of some stiff material that I've never seen before. It chafes my skin. Where did he get these unwieldy things, anyway?

Suddenly I think about the oblong tube I found in Elizabet's bag, the one that gave off that bright bluish light. The same kind that the Ring-Guards used to find me and Jasper in the dead of night. Is the Triad *using* some of their Relics instead of studying and Chronicling them? Do the boots date from the Healing? If so, why aren't they on a display shelf in the Hall of Archons or on a table in the Conservation Chamber rather than on my feet, where they don't belong?

But I can't ask any of this. Not without tipping my hand. And not without breaking the unquestioning authority that all Archons must vow to obey.

I glance over at the two other Archons training with me. I recognize them both—Henrik and Alexei. They won the two Testing years before mine. They nod in my direction, but don't acknowledge me otherwise. Maybe they're as stumped as everyone else as to how to greet a fellow Archon who a few short months ago was just another Maiden. Or maybe they don't care at all. After all, they are struggling with the boots, too. The masked Archon has ordered them up the ice wall more times than he has ordered me.

It seems that we will have to repeat the exercise until we get the hang of these boots.

"Give me my bear claws any day," I overhear Henrik hiss at Alexei.

"I know," Alexei whispers. "Why are they making us try these—"

"Do I hear talking?" the masked Archon shouts from his watching post.

"No, Archon Valteri," they yell back, almost in unison.

Valteri. It sounds familiar, but I don't know why. I can't link the name to a face or a particular story from my father.

The snow crunches under the Archon's feet as he marches over to the two boys. "Do you think this is a joke?"

"No, Archon Valteri," they answer together.

"Because I assure you that I am not kidding." He circles them like a hawk. "I want you both to climb to the summit. No ropes. No axes. Just those boots. And stay there until the Midday Bell. That'll stop your grumbling."

They are silent in response. I can feel their fear of the Archon and of his punishment.

"What, no smart remarks now? The vow of the Archon requires complete *pareo*. I expect that in the future, you will submit to your superiors' will without hesitation and without comment. Or I will mete out far worse."

"Yes, Archon Valteri," they respond, their voices one yet again.

He stares at them. "What are you waiting for? Get up there!"

Henrik and Alexei scramble to the base of the ice wall and start their ascent. For a tick, I am mesmerized by their clumsy efforts to climb without the usual tools. I can't imagine making it to the top without my axes, ropes, and ice screws; in fact, I might not even be able to reach the crest. Then I realize Valteri is staring at me, and I start climbing as well.

"What are you doing, Archon Eva?"

"You told me to scale the wall again, Archon Valteri."

"True." He pauses. "I'm glad that at least one of my trainees is listening. But we will leave the other two to their penance."

"Yes, Archon Valteri." What shall I do instead? The Yard contains other training exercises—trenches with frozen-in artifacts for excavations and tunnels to practice fortification-building—but Valteri has not ordered me to those works. If nothing else today, I've learned the lesson about obedience. So I stay where I am.

"Come on. It is nearly the Terce Bell, in any event. Archon Theo awaits."

He starts walking toward the Yard's only entry point. His stride is quick, and I must run to keep pace. I hear him muttering under his breath. "The hubris . . ."

Inside the entryway, Theo does indeed await. After the men half-bow to each other, Valteri reaches up to pull off his mask. I stifle a gasp. Half of Valteri's face is sheared off. He wears a mask not because he is unusually sensitive to the cold, but to protect what's left of his face. That's why I know his name, though I've never seen him before. My father has mentioned him. He's mysterious, rumored never to leave the Hall. His entire existence is devoted solely to training new Archons.

"I'll expect you after the Prime Bell tomorrow, Archon Eva," Valteri says. He vanishes into the warren of hallways surrounding the Yard.

"You were staring at his face," Theo comments as he leads me down another corridor.

"No, Archon Theo. I was just—"

"Please don't give me excuses. I saw you."

Theo's voice is stern, almost condemning, and my stomach lurches. Is he going to punish me as Valteri punished Henrik and Alexei? "I'm sorry, Arch—"

"I'm not chastising you, Archon Eva. It's normal to gawk. There's no one else like him in the Aerie, and not many have seen his face since he stays in the Hall. Thank the Gods. Do you know what happened to him?"

"No." I'd heard stories about an accident—not from Father—so I am interested in Theo's version of the truth.

"On his first excavation after the Testing, his rope gave out. He fell over a hundred feet down the base of a glacier. He slid past an icy outcropping imbedded with rock, and it sliced off his ear, cheek, eye, and half his nose. As you saw."

"By the Gods." The phrase just slips out. A similar accident could've easily happened to me. Or any other Testor.

"Feel no pity for Archon Valteri. The Gods gave him a new calling when They took away his face. They gifted him with the purpose of training new Archons in the nuances of climbing so that the tragedy that befell him does not befall them. The harshness you see from him toward the trainees stems from the motives of a zealot."

I nod guiltily. I feel sorry that I recoiled from Valteri. How strong he must be to devote his life to keeping other Testors safe, and how comforting for him to believe that the Gods are the architects of his fate. I wish my own faith was so certain.

Instead, I am left questioning my own convictions while at the same time having to believe in my own ability to control the future. I can't help thinking that Lukas would admire Valteri, too. They have much in common. It would be so much easier to be a zealot.

IX.

Junius 25
Year 242, A.H.

" To the Vaults, Archon Eva. We do not want to be late for the Scribe. He runs a tight ship." Theo suddenly sounds impatient with me. Tight ship? What in the Gods does that mean?

I strip off my climbing gear, absurd boots, and outer layer of hides, and hand them to an Attendant, relieved to slip on my beloved *kamiks*. Wearing only my uniform of black sealskin tunic, coat, leggings, and *kamiks*, I walk alongside Theo toward the staircase. As he describes the precautions taken by the Scribe to preserve the records which I must studiously follow during my investigation, I hear a scream from the Yard.

We race to one of the arched cutouts.

Henrik has fallen down the side of the ice and clings

to the ice wall by a single hand. How he found one of the scant handholds, I don't know. Alexei, who has somehow managed to reach the peak, stares down at Henrik, clearly considering whether he should descend to help him.

"Don't," Henrik shouts up at him.

Alexei holds his position, thighs quaking with the effort of staying steady. I doubt Alexei would be much use to Henrik anyway; he looks weak. Theo and I watch as Henrik creeps toward the top. His progress is slow, with missteps and slips. But Theo motions for us to move on.

I'm not so willing to leave. "What happens if Henrik doesn't make it to the top? Shouldn't we stay to make sure they're safe?"

Theo shrugs, but I see his face. The plight of Alexei and Henrik disturbs him. Still, he says, "You heard Archon Valteri's punishment orders. Henrik and Alexei must stay at the top until the Midday Bell. It isn't the Midday Bell, is it?"

"So they must reach the summit and stay there for nearly three more bells—accident or not?" I blurt out, without thinking. I should be more circumspect; I sound as if I'm challenging Valteri's decision.

Theo's gaze meets mine. "I read the reports from the Testing, and I know your history, Archon Eva. You know The Lex as well as any Lexor. Think on it. What does The Lex say about Archons who do not follow the orders of their seniors?"

The Lex sets forth a panoply of punishments for Triad members who fail to abide by orders—from expulsion from the Triad ranks, to exile in the Boundary lands, to execution. Valteri could have been much harsher with Henrik and Alexei. But surely, they don't follow The Lex to the letter in practice? Especially in training exercises?

I wish my father was here. He wouldn't let this happen. Or would he? He is the Chief Archon; this is his Hall in a way. I can't imagine much happens without his approval. There's so much he hasn't told me. There is a side I don't know of him, perhaps many sides. But how can I fault him? We are all keeping secrets.

Theo takes me by the elbow. "Eva, this matter is not for us. The Gods have other work for you to do. More important work."

He is right, though not in the way he believes. Taking a deep breath, I glance out at the Yard one last time. Henrik continues to eke his way up the ice wall. I turn away and follow Theo to the Vault. I must.

The climb up the Hall of Archons' only staircase seems easy after my morning in the Yard. We reach another pair of solidly built Archon-Guards protecting the doors at the top. Theo says to them, "This is Archon Eva. She will have need of the Vault. You will allow her access."

"Yes, Archon Theo," they answer.

We pass under the doorway to the Vault. All at once I'm inside the brightest, most airy space I've ever seen. The walls soar toward a point at the center, illuminated and decorated by countless ice-windows. Crowded shelves border the room, and I feel giddy thinking about the treasures I might find on them. Lukas would be so thrilled at my good fortune.

Lukas. I wonder where he is right now.

A throat clearing brings me back to the present. The Vault Scribe sits at the center of this vast chamber like a spider in his lair. The wrinkles of his dour face even resemble the intricate pattern of a spiderweb and look almost as welcoming.

Theo makes our introductions, but the Scribe—an

Archon, but with a particular Lex-given task—isn't one for conversation. Once Theo tells him the excavation in which we are interested, the Scribe wordlessly leads us to a set of shelves in the farthest corner of the chamber.

"You will find what you need here," he says, the first words he's uttered since we've entered.

The shelves overflow with leather-bound books, rolled parchments, and stacks of papers. There's even a leather pouch that I'm guessing holds tiny scrolls sent back by bird from expeditions. I don't think any of these documents will inch me closer to my true work, but the thought that Madeline might have written some of these words has me itching to pore through them.

"Just these four shelves?" Theo asks.

"These are the only records left from that excavation."

"A scant few. Most digs have an entire bank's worth of papers."

The Scribe sniffs. "The last Scribe was not one for scrupulous conservation. We lost many during his tenure."

"Is the Vault organized chronologically?" I ask. I'm wondering where I might locate the really early documents. The ones I talked about with Lukas. It's a question that Lukas would want me to ask. I feel like I'm always carrying on a conversation with him internally, like I did when I was beyond the Ring in the Testing.

The Scribe shifts his gaze to me. "Why do you ask? You will have no need of documents other than the ones on these four shelves." His voice is inhospitable at best.

Stupid, Eva, stupid. I just drew his attention to me in the worst way possible. "Just curious, Scribe. My apologies."

Theo shoots me an inscrutable look. "An eager young Archon, Scribe. She'll keep within her boundaries."

I know that Theo is protecting me. Why, though? Even though Theo seems an ally and genuine Mentor, I know I must be wary of him—of everyone except Lukas. After all, Laurence hand-picked Theo for me.

I bow to them both. "Of course I will. I'm sorry if my question suggested otherwise."

My access to the Vault will not be as unfettered as I'd hoped. With the sharp-eyed Scribe's gaze upon me, it will be even harder than I imagined to find the documents Lukas needs me to uncover.

X.

Junius 25 through Julius 6
Year 242, A.H.

My days training in the Hall of Archons assume a certain shape and structure. They become almost predictable. I only wish that the rest of my life was so certain.

Mornings I spend in the Yard, experimenting with unusual equipment on the ice wall, tunneling into the ice cave to practice fortifications, and chiseling out artifacts from all manner of ice formations. After nibbling on some dried fish and spending a bell or two in the Conservation Chamber or the Chamber of Maps, I race to the Vault. There I lose myself in the past.

Most days, I'm alone in my schooling, with only senior Archons Theo and Valteri for company. Henrik and Alexei appear occasionally, allaying my worst fears about their punishment, but I guess the other Archons are busy in their chambers or on digs. I never see my father after he leads the morning prayer, but I feel the presence of the Chief everywhere.

Trying my best to ignore the watchful eyes of the Scribe, who's beginning to look more like a vigilant, unblinking owl than a spider, I examine the scraps of paper on my designated shelves. They contain a treasure trove of maps of the excavation Site, grids of the crevasse digs, detailed journal entries of the artifacts found by Testors, and Chronicles. The bells spring by at a husky's pace as I reconstruct history.

Whenever I return home at the *Vespers* bell, I feel as disoriented as my first day back from the Testing. It's hard to shift from working as an Archon recreating a hundred-year-old dig to the role of Maiden in dinner gowns, but day by day I'm becoming more masterful at the transition. I share with my eager mother what I can, but revert to the banal dinner conversation of my upbringing, as I'm ever mindful that Archons are barred from talking about the inner workings of the Hall or planned excavations. Such matters are considered too sensitive for Aerie people's ears, especially the Ladies and Maidens.

Funny, I guess that rule doesn't apply to me. I'm both Archon and Maiden, so in some ways I am neither.

I have no wish to be torn away from the records of old to accompany the unpleasant Laurence on a frigid dig on the Frozen Shores. I am loathe for the final day in the Hall to end. But it must.

"This is likely where the Founder's ship landed." Theo points to a spot on the map I've drawn, around which I've laid out all the Relic finds from Madeline's Testing year in a circle. He is pleased with the grid I've superimposed over the Site map.

"The Founder's ship?" My voice quivers with excitement. No one has mentioned it as the purpose for my investigation or for this dig. If Theo is right, then I have mapped out a most critical find. The Archons have long sought the precise location of the only Founders' ship never found—and with it, the exact place where the Gods commanded our Founders to land during the Healing. A most Holy Site. If you believe in the Gods and The Lex, that is.

"Yes," he answers, a smug little smile appearing on his face.

"How can you tell?" I ask.

He puffs up a little. It's the signal that he's about to lecture me on some important point. Even though I'm still wary of Theo, I've learned much from him, so I prepare myself to listen with care.

"The Relics you've marked in this circle all bear the same ice and water marks. Those marks show us that these artifacts froze here in situ, and did not simply wash upon the Frozen Shores and freeze there after traveling a long distance in the Healing like so many other Relics. If I am correct in this—and I'm certain that I am—the Relics had to come from the same place. The only possible place is a ship. A Founder's ship."

"What an astounding discovery this would be," I reply. "Are you certain?"

He crosses his arms and rests them on his generous belly. It's been many years since Theo subjected himself to the rigors of a dig. At first, I think he is going to chastise me for questioning him. *Pareo* is my duty, after all. But then that little smile appears again. "My dear girl, the Relics themselves tell us the story, if we only know how to look and listen . . ."

As he explains the scientific clues that give rise to his conclusion, I'm reminded of Elizabet. The Relics I found in her pack told me a story, too, one that I Chronicled. But the tale I thought they told turned out to be very different than Elizabet's true history. I must remain mindful of that now as I listen to Theo's understanding of the past.

But Theo abruptly stops. "This reminds me of another dig that was unexpectedly closed when the ice shifted. Scribe?" he calls out.

I watch his ambling toward the table of the Scribe, who in turn sits and watches me, as he has day after day with those unblinking eyes. His gaze never needs to move; no one else has entered the Vault since I began coming here.

"Can you find me the maps from the Testing of 126 A.H.?" Theo asks. "I think they might prove quite useful here."

The two men approach another set of shelves, leaving me alone for a tick. I sift through the documents on the table and decide to review a small leather book that sits among the unexamined records from the Testing of 102 A.H. With my gloved hand, I turn the little book this way and that. It reminds me of Eamon's journal in shape and size. The book is well-worn, and the back cover has fallen off, taking with it several pages. Nervous that I might cause further damage, I open to the first page slowly.

Words materialize. Something about them, something unusual, almost indescribable, catches my attention. Soon I realize that it isn't the words themselves.

No, it's the way the words are written. The handwriting

looks like that of a Maiden. In School, Maidens and Gallants are taught to form letters with subtle differences; most Schoolchildren wouldn't even notice this unless they had a twin of the opposite sex. Like me and Eamon.

The only female on this dig was Madeline. This must be her journal, even though I do not see her name anywhere on the pages. A sudden compulsion overtakes me, and I crane my neck to see what Theo and the Scribe are doing. Then I slip the journal under my tunic.

XI.

Julius 6
Year 242, A.H.

I race down the streets. By the time I make it through the front door and into the Feast room, my father is already incanting the Lex prayer for meals, "Hail Mother, Full of Grace, the Father is with thee . . ." Oh, no, the Feast has already begun. I have no choice but to attend it in my Archon uniform.

I slink into the room and settle into my seat. Wincing at the noise my chair makes as I shimmy into it, I quickly arrange my hands in a prayerful pose. As if I'd been present since the start of the meal, I utter the sacred words along with everyone else at the table. "Blessed art Thou . . ."

I keep my head bowed low as The Lex requires, but manage to sneak a peek around the table. Who have my parents invited to the last family meal before I leave for my first excavation as Archon? My aunts and uncles with their children. Jasper, of course, and his parents along with him. It wouldn't be a Feast without my Betrothed. The gathering looks remarkably like the one before I left for the Testing, except Lukas isn't lining the wall with the rest of the Boundary Attendants. Although I try hard not to think about Lukas with Jasper so near, it's impossible.

When my father finishes the prayer, he gives me a displeased glance but makes no comment about my late arrival. Of course my mother noticed it as well, but she's too busy resuming a conversation with my aunt about the design of my Union gown. A Maiden is usually very involved in the sewing and embroidering of the ice-blue gown worn on her wedding day—and even spends months with family and friends at the hearth stitching away on the precious cloth created just for that occasion—but I haven't had a spare tick for such work. Not that my mother minds having full control over the gown.

In true Lady Margret fashion, the Feast begins with a splendid array of roasted fowl and bison, delicate late-spring vegetables from the Ark, and a hearty circular loaf of bread meant to symbolize the Mother. The meal finishes with sweets. I ignore the honey cakes. The banter is light and hopeful—so different from the night before the Testing. I think I'm the only one who feels dark, though I'm smiling.

I notice Jasper stealing looks at me when the attention of the table is absorbed by the banter of one guest or another. I know he's anxious about my departure; he's said as much in our rare private moments. To assuage him, I catch his eye and smile. I need him calm and unquestioning.

At the Feast's end, my parents and I line up at the door

to say our farewells and receive everyone's blessings. Jasper is last in line—on purpose, I'm certain. His parents wait just outside the door, shivering in the cold darkness, but he waves them on. "I'll be home in a few ticks."

Despite The Lex's mandates about chaperoning the Betrothed, my parents excuse themselves under the guise of checking on the Attendants—a task my father has never, ever undertaken. It's a silly ruse. I can't believe my mother has persuaded him to leave us alone. And that makes me nervous, too. She must have her own reasons. I wonder if she also sees the love in Jasper's eyes. I wonder if she hopes it will make me more a Lady and less an Archon.

Jasper and I stand together, hand in hand, under the archway to the door. It's the first time we've been alone since he waited for me at the base of the Ring.

"When will you return?" he asks.

"I haven't been given a date. I'll send word by hawk when I do."

"I would appreciate that. It will help with the waiting." He smiles a little. "Of course, all the work I have to do to prepare for the Forge will keep me distracted. I can't help but think that, with all your knowledge of The Lex, you're the one who would've made a wonderful Lexor. Not me."

I smile back, but it's bittersweet. "Well, the decision to try for the Archon Laurels wasn't by choice. That was by necessity."

"I know." He pauses, and his face grows serious. "Please take care, Eva."

"I will. I promise."

He lines up our hands. Finger to finger, thumb to thumb. His hands look so much bigger than mine. They're softer and less scarred compared to Lukas's.

Lukas. I'm thinking of him again, though I shouldn't be.

Jasper pulls me close. The length of our bodies touch, and he wraps his arms around me like the warmest cloak. I feel his breath upon me, and his heart beats fast. I wonder if he can feel mine racing, too.

I've imagined this moment many times since I called him my Betrothed the night at the Ring. I care about Jasper and respect him, but I had braced myself for the worst when it came to actually being private with him in a Maidenly way. I thought that the guilt I experience over deceiving him about my true Archon goals would make me feel awkward in his arms.

I was wrong.

He brings his face to mine. His eyes close, and he leans in to kiss me. I surrender to the unexpected softness of his lips and feel something spark within me. Something more than I felt that one night with Lukas. Much more. How can I feel like this with Jasper when I felt something with Lukas, too? I guess that I'm no Lex Maiden. But that is something that I already knew, isn't it?

Our lips start to part, and my heart beats more quickly. I lean into him, but he pulls back.

My eyelids flutter open. His brow is furrowed, his eyes flickering over my tunic.

I press my fingers to my lips. Did I do something wrong? I've never kissed a Gallant before.

Jasper's cheeks turn bright red. "I am so sorry, Eva. I can't believe I ruined this moment. Something jabbed me."

My cheeks are red, too, and I feel flustered. What in the Gods is he talking about? Did I poke him accidentally? And then I feel the outside of my tunic and remember.

It's Madeline's journal.

I'm furious with myself. How could I have been so simple-minded as to keep Madeline's journal under my tunic all night? Why didn't I just excuse myself at dinner and hide it somewhere in my room? But I know the answer. I had no idea I'd be in such close proximity with anyone before I retired.

"What have you got hiding under there, Eva?" Jasper's tone is playful, even flirtatious.

I figure playing along is my best gambit. "Just a book where I write down my thoughts."

He draws closer to me again. "What thoughts?"

"Maidenly thoughts." I answer in my best impression of Maidenly coquettishness.

"Not Archon thoughts?" He draws even closer. So close I can feel his warm breath on my cheeks.

"Not a single one."

He wraps his arms around me again. "Any thoughts about me?"

"Maybe," I whisper, and allow myself to be enveloped by his strong arms. He smells good, like evergreens and a roaring fire and something else. Something exclusively Jasper. His hands travel down my back slowly, and I shiver. For a tick, I forget that I'm pretending.

His hands slide under my tunic—an unimaginable, yet delicious, violation of The Lex—then he grabs the book. He's smiling playfully as if this is some Gallant-Maiden game, yet the action is so unlike Jasper that I am unprepared. I lunge for the book, but he's too quick. He's halfway across the room and flipping through the book before I catch up with him.

The smile vanishes. He stops flipping. "Why did you lie to me, Eva?"

"What do you mean?" I know what he means, but I'm buying time. The story I offered became unbelievable the moment he saw the obviously worn pages, but how can I explain what the book is without explaining how I came by it?

I reach for the journal, and he doesn't resist when I take it from his hands. His brows furrow in confusion and disappointment. "Eva, I saw the date on those pages. That book was written in year 98, after the Healing. It's no journal of yours."

"I'm sorry, Jasper." And I am. I don't to want pull him into my double life—I've already exposed him to so much—but what are my choices? "I was scared to tell you the truth."

His eyes narrow, and his jaw clenches. He asks a question much bigger than he could possibly know. "What is the truth, Eva?"

"It's the journal of the first female Testor, Madeline."

"Madeline? The one you used in your Lex arguments to be allowed to Test?"

"Yes."

"How did you come by this?"

"From the Archon Hall," I say, as if this could explain my possession.

"I wouldn't think that such a precious, delicate document would be allowed to leave the Hall of Archons. Or the Library."

"It wasn't."

"Is that why it's under your tunic?"

"Yes."

"Because you took it."

"Yes. Although they don't realize that it's Madeline's journal."

He winces. "You took it without permission."

"Yes." No sense mincing words.

He steps away from me. "I can't believe you stole this. You could end up in shackles or worse. The Gallows have been used for far less serious Lex violations."

"I know."

"Why did you take such a risk? You worked so hard to become an Archon. To fulfill Eamon's dream for him. How many times did I hear you say that? Why in the Gods would you endanger that victory now?"

Should I chance another lie and tell him that I felt compelled to steal the journal because Madeline is my spirit-mate? From my references to her in my sessions with the Lexors, he knows how I treasure her history and her legacy. He might believe me. But Jasper deserves better. And I'm so sick of lying to everyone. Everyone except Lukas.

"Do you remember the conversation we had next to the fire the night before we came back from the Testing?"

"Yes." That night we shared with each other our darkest thoughts about The Lex and the Testing and New North. It was the first night I thought that maybe I could enter a Union with him. Not just because everyone else wanted it to happen. Because I could talk to him more honestly than anyone except Lukas.

"I've only had a chance to skim over a few pages, but I think Madeline might have felt the way we feel. I think she might have known something about the creation of The Lex. The creation of New North, even. I felt duty bound to take the journal and follow up on some of her concerns."

His face softens, but he doesn't move closer to me. "Why would you be scared to tell me that, Eva? You know I share your doubts. Anyway, as your Betrothed, I promise that you can trust me with any of your truths."

"Really?" I ask. How I wish it could be true. But if Jasper actually knew the nature of *all* my truths, I don't think he'd make such promises. He might not even want a Union.

"Really."

I walk closer to him. Taking a most unMaidenly step, I wrap my arms around him. I will try to trust him, but I'll need to be careful. I can't endanger him. I need him on my side. "I will never doubt you again," I say.

He leans toward me, and I allow my lips to touch his.

XII.

Julius 7
Year 242, A.H.

This leave-taking is so different than the last. No throngs of Aerie and Boundary gather round the Gate to say farewell: just a phalanx of Archons, Scouts, Boundary Climbers, and Attendants—and, of course, our huskies. No tearful hugs from family members, or calls of luck from neighbors and friends, or long embraces from a Betrothed. No pageantry like the Testing, just a smudge of black heading into the immense whiteness.

We start on a route different than that of the Testing, one that bears none of the challenges, either. Seeming to sense my uncertainties, Archon Theo calls, "We save all the danger for the dig," but I'm not appeased; all I can see is a well-worn groove in the ice that serves as a road. No sudden dips, no change from pack ice to *quiasuqaq*, no unexpected crevasses. No dangerous wilds from the tales told by Schoolteachers to their students. Just a pathway traveled by Archons for centuries.

Laurence leads our group. Six Archons, twelve Scouts, and twenty-four Boundary folk, these latter charged with the heaviest loads. Theo was probably more shocked than our fellow Archons to be included in this expedition; his presence must have something to do with mine. Did my father command Theo to accompany us? He didn't tell me, and as Chief Archon, he is somehow more distant than ever. More proof that I cannot have an answer to things at which I can only guess. I must focus on what I can know.

With our huskies, we will be a team of forty-two, charged with excavating one of the most precious sites in all of New North. On all of His Earth. No one says it, but the anticipation is heavy in the air. Frozen, like icicles.

The morning is bright and clear, and instead of sinking into my dark thoughts, I try to relax into the rhythm of the ride. My dogs are delighted to be free from the Aerie walls, and I concentrate on their joyousness. Certainly I'm happy to be reunited with Indica, Johan, James, Singerneq, Rasmus, Pierre, and Akim after so many days confined to the Archon Hall. But I miss Sigurd, my lone female, the one who died on the Testing journey. The team seems incomplete without her.

I miss Jasper out here as well. The last time I ventured beyond the Ring, Jasper rode alongside me . . .

I draw in a sharp breath. I am lying to myself. I'd ventured out beyond the Ring since the Testing—with Lukas. But I cannot linger on that memory, not here.

The landscape looks different than any I've seen. The warmer weather of summer melts the glaciers surrounding us, creating waterfalls in the crevices between them. These rushing, sparkling stripes seem numerous, but I've seen no other summer season outside the Aerie with which to compare them. The evergreens, plentiful and bright green against the white-grey of the icescape, jut out toward Her Sun. Birds chirp from nests within.

To my great surprise, we reach the Frozen Shores long before the Sun begins Her descent.

The journey is so brief that I realize the Site must sit at the Shore point closest to the Aerie. Interesting. Although I'd spent weeks mapping and gridding the Site—and obviously saw the Site's proximity to my home—I'd never thought of the true distance before. If the Site indeed contains one of the Founders' ships, the journey by the Founders to the Aerie would have been short. As short as Madeline's journey *should* have been in her Testing.

All at once, I am angry. The truth confirms my doubts about the necessity of the Testing hardship. I suspect the sacrifices were empty—those of every Testor, including me and Madeline. I grow more furious thinking about the descriptions in Madeline's journal of her Testing—the long, hungry, freezing *siniks*, the Testor injuries and deaths. All for nothing. Jasper would be horrified to learn this, too, though we had suspected as much during our short trip to the Aerie at the end of the Testing.

I look for the signal from Archon Laurence to make camp, but he doesn't give it.

While I wait, I dismount briefly to rub down my tired dogs. We've traveled a much smaller distance than I thought we would, but the dogs are tired. I reach into my pack for some oil to massage their feet and triceps and biceps where their harnesses chafe them. Then I throw them some dried meat.

Still Laurence doesn't give the signal. He gathers two of the other Archons to his side, and they nod while Laurence gesticulates. His wild movements show anger. But instead of worrying about what in the Gods they're discussing, I stare out at the Frozen Seas. We are so close to the edge of the Frozen Shores that I can see where the coast meets the sea.

The water is clear, cerulean blue, except where the blue-green of the shoreline's glacial runoff meets the sea. Hundreds of small icebergs bob playfully in the seawaters, while an enormous one lurks nearby like a protective mother. Sea lions and their pups sun themselves in Her rays on the flat tops of these icy masses, each one a different shade of blue—silver, sky, stone, or aqua—depending on the concentration of ice.

Despite everything I've suffered to get here, I feel lucky to have the privilege to gaze upon this beautiful sight with my own eyes. Even though we live on an island, very few non-Boundary people in New North have actually seen the sea. Only Archons and those Testors who vied for the Laurels, like Jasper, have witnessed firsthand the waters that changed our world.

Laurence waves the two Archons away and motions instead for Theo to come over and study the document he's pulled from his bag. The two men appear to argue until Theo crooks his finger for me to join them. My heart starts beating fast, even though I've been motionless for long ticks.

I hitch my dog team to an icy outcropping and walk to Theo's side. I stay close to him, as if his girth could shelter me from the wrath brewing within Laurence.

Laurence brings his face—ice-crusted beard and all—close to mine. His breath smells of dried fish, and his voice brims with anger. "Exactly where would you recommend we dig, Archon Eva?" He spits out my name as if it's a curse and stabs his gloved finger on the red circle at the center of the map in his other hand. My map and my red circle, the one over which I labored. "The designated Site on your precious map sits on an empty ice-field. Not on the crevasse we expected to be here."

I glance down at the map and then stare out at the ice-field.

This Site hasn't been excavated—or possibly even properly gridded—in over a century; of course, the icescape has changed. Still, studying the Site, I can't help but smile. So many of the Aerie are so blind. Maybe it's their lack of language that hinders their sight. I mean, can you really understand all the types of snow and ice if you don't have a name for each, as do the Boundary?

"Why in the Gods are you smiling, Archon Eva? It's no laughing matter to drag a team of forty-two out to an empty Site."

The smile disappears from my lips. My heart beats even faster, and my stomach churns. I decide that if Laurence senses my fear, he will win the battle he's staging against me. I've worked too hard in my brother's name to stumble so easily, so I square my shoulders and look straight into the Archon's ice-crusted face. "This ice-field isn't as empty as you think." I stretch out my hand. "May I have the map, Archon Laurence?"

He opens his mouth wide as if to scream, then snaps it shut and shoves the map into my hand. "Very well. Go dig your own icy grave."

Map in hand, all eyes on me, I walk the circle I etched. I note the change in the color and depth and texture of the ice, as Lukas taught me over and over how to do during my Testing training. I think over Madeline's detailed descriptions in the journal I stole. I squat over a particularly blue stretch, take off my gloves, run my hands along the snow, close my eyes, and then stand up.

"Right here. This is where we should dig," I say as I put my gloves back on.

Silence. Raised eyebrows. And a lone chortle. That's all the response I get. I know what they're waiting for: Laurence's judgment.

After a long, long tick, he strides over to me, crosses his arms, and booms, "You are certain this is the spot?" The question isn't for me; it's for everyone else.

I hold my ground. "Yes."

"Are you willing to bet your Archon Laurels?"

He's going to make me risk everything. What are my choices? It would come to this sooner or later.

"Yes," I repeat. "This is where you'll find the ship."

The team is still; we all await Archon Laurence's reaction. Will he act on my pronouncement, or will he punish me for my audacity? The ticks seem long, and the words from the first page of Madeline's journal pass through my mind. They are fitting.

Journal of Madeline
Aprilus 7 Year 98, A.H.

The Archons were right to focus on the discipline of our minds during training for the Testing. If they had not—if I had let my mind soften like so many Gallants and Maidens who live only within the comfort and protective embrace of the Aerie—J would not have survived this Tundra of treeless, foodless, freezing, barren ice flats. J would have turned my dog team around and headed home. Or J would have succumbed to the icy fingers of death.

But J prevail. J am now four days into the blinding white of Mother Sun's reflected rays. J am also three days into utter solitude without a single sighting of a fellow Testor and two days past food, for J am ungifted at hunting. What remains of my dried food stores J must give to my huskies, for without them J will certainly die.

To turn my thoughts away from the sharp pains of hunger stabbing my gut and the gnawing worry eating away my mind, J conjure up the Archons' teaching. Pray to Father Earth, as they instructed us. Over and over and over. Pray that He spares me, as He spared my people . . .

At last, J reach the Testing Site. J see that the arduous journey was necessary. Jt purified my spirit for the sacred task of excavation. Fasting, suffering, praying, The Lex says these are necessary for the purification of our spirits, and what is the Testing but fasting, suffering, and praying?

J pray that my spirit is cleansed of the defilement of Apple and his minions, such that the Gods deem me worthy of finding a Relic.

XIII.

Julius 7–8
Year 242, A.H.

"We will excavate here!" Archon Laurence calls out to the group, then marches away.

I sigh in relief.

The Boundary workers rush to dismount and unpack their bags. I watch as they bring out picks and axes and start digging into the spot where I'm practically standing. I step back. When one Boundary Climber pulls out a grey metal tube from his pack and sets it aflame, I am transfixed as the ice just melts away. I am also sickened. If the Testors had devices such as these during the Testing, the ritual might have taken bells instead of *siniks*. No one need have died.

I glance over at Theo, the question probably obvious in my eyes: What is the unusual device? It looks like

something excavated during a Testing, like those awful
boots Valteri made us use.

He shrugs, conveying nothing. Maybe he doesn't even
suspect that the device is another piece of Tech from pre-
Healing days. Tech that's not so evil, after all. I wonder if
he even understands that these devices *are* Tech; his faith in
The Lex seems too strong to accommodate any real understanding.

The Boundary worker uses the fire-wielding tube to melt
snow very quickly. I'm so mesmerized that I don't even
move for nearly a quarter bell. Finally, when I realize I'm
the only one of the forty-two standing still, I hustle over to
my dog team and feed them from my stores. Gods forbid I
appear lazy: Industry and vigor are what the Gods demand
in this, our second chance.

I board my sled and start to guide my team toward the
campsite nearby—where the Archons are either building *iglus* or watching the Boundary workers dig—when I
make a decision. I will not stand idly by and watch as other
human beings excavate the spot that I've Claimed. This is
my responsibility, my call, and everything is on the line.

I will join them. Nothing in The Lex forbids it.

AFTER I HITCH UP my dogs at the camp, I return to the Site.
In the midst of the Boundary workers, I plunge my pick
into the ice and drag it in the circular shape I had inscribed
on the map. Since I don't have the fire-wielders that the
Boundary folk do, I assist in the best way I can: I mark
the exact location of the ship. The Boundary workers do
not acknowledge me with words, but I see their sidelong
glances, and they move out of my way in respect. Much as
Lukas and Jasper would do if they were here.

A figure moves in my peripheral vision, and I look up to see Theo waddling over to me. Breathing heavily, he bends down to where I'm continuing to mark a circle in the frozen surface. "What are you doing, Archon Eva?"

"What does it look like?" I whisper back.

"This is not your place."

"I don't have any other."

"Eva, you don't want the other Archons to think of you as Boundary. They're already struggling with thinking of a Maiden as Archon—and of the Chief's daughter. Don't throw Boundary into the already confusing mix."

It's the first time he's mentioned this issue. I know he's trying to be kind, and I know he's taking a risk by helping me and showing his solidarity. Especially by stating the real issues aloud. But I have to stay firm. "Archon Theo, I appreciate all you've done to help me so far, but I must carve out my own place." I continue working to drive the point home.

"Archon Eva, you need to think of your reputation."

I stand up. "I won't have much of a reputation if I get this spot wrong, will I? And I won't have any Archon Laurels, either."

Theo stares at me. "I suppose you are right."

He waits a tick to see if I'll waver, and when I don't, he totters back to the campsite. My spirits sink a little with every step he takes. I've just rejected the only ally I've got out here. But I remind myself that I'm not really alone. Jasper and Lukas wait for me. And I have the spirits and memories of Eamon and Elizabet and Madeline to spur me on when the bells get bleak, though memories are cold company.

Even when the Sun finishes Her descent, the Boundary

workers' fire-wielders provide light enough to continue, and they don't stop working. I can hear the other Archons finishing up with their *iglus*, eating their evening meal, and readying for rest. I refuse to lay down my pick until the Boundary workers finally stop, too.

As I follow them back to the camp and survey possible *iglu* locations, I realize that the only ground left for them—for all of us, actually—to build shelter is an exposed stretch of ice. I can't help but think that this is part of Laurence's retribution against me—for being a Maiden, for daring to become an Archon, for standing up to him before the entire team, and worst of all, for being the Chief's daughter. Even if I weren't his daughter, my father would be furious at Laurence's behavior, but he's not out here. It's just me, and I won't yield to Laurence.

Instead, I pledge to make the sturdiest *iglu* ever. I will place it right between the Archon and Boundary camps. It will be my silent message to Laurence that I received his little missive and am unshaken. Anyway, building my *iglu* in no-man's-land seems appropriate; I really don't fit into any one world. And I am no man.

I follow the Boundary workers as we search for *igluksaq,* the perfect snow for *iglu*-building. *Naneq* guiding my way through the dark *sinik,* I finally locate a large swath of dry, well-packed snow, the product of a single snowfall and therefore not likely to fracture when formed into blocks. I signal the Boundary workers to join me at the snow-mound near the Archons' side of the camp.

Side by side we carve out the snow-blocks for our *iglus*. With the cold of night and the frigid wind whipping off the glacier tops, it's hard labor. We never speak, but I sense a softening in their attitude toward me the longer we work.

I wonder if Lukas has any of them looking out for me, as he'd charged his uncle with doing during the Testing. Lukas's extended family—his *tuqslurausiit*—is large and could be anywhere.

In a few bells, our *iglus* are finished, our morning meal complete, and our equipment back out. By the time Her first light shines down on the camp and the Archons are beginning to stir, I am already hard at work at the Site.

I can't keep from smiling at the surprised look on the Archons' faces at the camp we've built and the hollow we've made in the Earth. All while they were sleeping.

The labor is intense, but I don't let myself yield. I won't let Laurence see me falter in any way. It takes bells for my perseverance to reap rewards.

But then I see it. The tip of the ship. Just like in Madeline's journal.

XIV.

Journal of Madeline
Aprilus 18 Year 98, A.H.

"Relic!"

J hear one of the other Testors call out his discovery. From the slight accent, which no one but a fellow french-speaker would detect, J know it's Pierre.

J glance up the wall of sheer ice from which J dangle, a perch that would have terrified me before the real ter-ror of the barren and blinding Tundra. Out here, it feels like Mother Sun never sets; she simply curtsies below the horizon. J dig my axe and the toe of my bear-claw boot into the wall and swing left on my sealskin rope. Pierre is several hundred handsbreadth above me. A Boundary Climber scales horizontally along the wall to Pierre's side.

"I think it's a cache of weapons," I hear Pierre say. Then he whispers, "Incroyable." Funny, what you can hear in this crevasse. Does he know I'm right below him? I'm not the only one clinging to the frenchspeak of home; it's really the only comfort we have left. I should be worried. Pre-Healing weaponry is a hugely important find, and Pierre is the fourth to make a Relic call. Every night, the other three Relic-holders scurry to their iglus to study their artifacts and start their Chronicles. The chance of winning the Archon Laurels starts to drift away from me.

So why am I at peace? Is it faith in the Gods, Mother Sun and Father Earth? Is it the training?

No. It stems from something else entirely. Somehow I believe that a critical Relic waits beneath the ice I've staked as my Claim. In fact, I've ignored artifacts much easier to dig out in favor of it. In the wavy grey ice covering my Relic, I see the powerful depth and texture of something massive. I pray to the Gods that this belief does not come from some magical trickery.

Here is where I steel my mind not to succumb to Vanity and ambition.

I push off the wall and descend away from Pierre, back

down my line into the chasm. I am the Testor with the deepest spot, and though I'm well used to cold, I feel the ice seep into my bones as soon as I take my position. I fire up my lamp, and the heat warms me a little. I watch as water trickles down the sheer side of the wall, though I dare not follow its trail with my eyes. Many chasms have no visible bottom, and Testors are taught to keep their eyes ahead. Those who ignored this advice in past Testings were never seen again.

I hurl my axe into the ice with all my strength, and a huge chunk flies off. A few more swings, and finally my efforts and patience are rewarded. A gaping hole opens in the wall.

My lamp in hand, I crawl inside. There's a gleam in the farthest reaches. I pull my chisel out of my belt and start chipping away at the crystalline sheath that obscures it. Without a scaffold to hold up the frozen ceiling, this work is dangerous, but I am powerless to stop. I must know what lies within this ice. I know that the final horn will sound soon, and that I must surface or spend the black night in this chasm. But how can I rise empty-handed?

My chisel clangs as I finally hit metal. I worry that the sound might echo through the chasm, alerting Pierre and every other Testor to my find. But I am too deep. I get down on all fours, chisel and pick in hand, furiously scraping away the final frost. In a single tick, a rush like the thunder of a summer storm, I understand what I've unearthed. I sit on my haunches and laugh, for this Relic is far more momentous than I ever imagined.

I am kneeling on the very tip of a ship. Not just any ship. The clang of metal has revealed a plate carved with a single gleaming word: Genesis. The vessel of the Founders. The vessel made holy by The Lex.

XV.

Julius 8–11
Year 242, A.H.

The grey metallic tip of the hull juts out from the ice. The sight sends everyone scrambling. Even the Archons grab picks, shovels, and fire-wielders and race to the gaping hole in the ice we carved out while they stood by and watched. I guess the wall between Archon and Boundary flattens in the wake of a Relic discovery like the *Genesis*.

Within a few bells, the outline of the entire deck begins to emerge. Just as Madeline described. Just as I etched in the ice. And just as I told Archon Laurence.

I try to stay humble. I try to remind myself that my goal isn't Archon glory but subversion. I am here to fulfill the objectives of my brother and Lukas. Still a subtle, almost indiscernible, shift in the mood occurs. Several of the

Archons, ones who'd been patently ignoring me up until now, nod in my direction as we dig. I hear the whispers of two compliments—a "Nice work, Archon Eva," and one "Good call"—as I pass by one section of the Site to grab another tool. Even Laurence gives me a wide berth. It feels good.

But the elation of that moment of discovery and whatever fleeting reverence the Archons doled out fades in the three *siniks* that follow. Even with forty-two trained excavators working in tireless shifts, the ship refuses to reveal itself beyond the deck. It seems that time and ice locked down on the ship just as the rest of the *Genesis* sank into the Frozen Seas during the Healing.

"I fear we have no choice but the bonfires," Laurence announces at the nightly shift-change meeting.

I hear grumbles from the Archons and the Boundary workers alike. No one likes to use the bonfires; they melt the snow too rapidly. Relics can get destroyed in the rush of water, or worse. The fast melt often makes the Site unstable, leading to injury and death.

I know how to unlock the *Genesis* without all that risk. But do I dare to say it?

Other ideas are offered, ones I know will not yield the *Genesis* treasure. Ones that may well destroy our access to it forever.

I decide to enter the fray. "We have another choice," I say. My voice wavers a little.

"Oh, really? Based on your vast experience at excavations?" Archon Laurence asks. He pauses dramatically and raises an eyebrow. His exaggerated expression gets the laugh he wanted, but I see the weakness in his sarcasm.

"The door. We need to dig out the door." So far I've kept

quiet about any details I learned from Madeline's journal; I don't want to call any undue attention to my unusual knowledge. But if I don't take this gamble, our only choice will be the bonfires.

"What in the Gods are you talking about, Archon Eva?" Laurence's old fury resurfaces. Since I accurately identified the Site, he has been tolerant of me, though hardly respectful, and that's only because the other Archons voiced their approval. But after three *siniks* without much progress, he can't help himself.

"The ship has been frozen into the ice in a near-vertical position. We were able to loosen the ice around the deck, but then we hit a solid mass. That ice is frozen around the frame of a door. A door connecting the deck to a cabin. I suspect that the cabin itself is not ice-locked." I hold my breath for a moment, hoping the explanation was sufficient to sidestep the unspoken question of how I know the layout of the ship.

Laurence laughs again as if my idea is preposterous. But the laugh rings hollow, and the grumbling intensifies. The men want any alternative to the bonfires, and he can't afford to ignore me. "How do you know that? Did the Gods send you a message?"

I decide to take seriously his last attempt at a demeaning joke. Nobody likes sacrilege, and I might win a few Boundary Climbers or Archons to my side if I play into it. "Maybe, Archon Laurence. The Lex says that the Gods do work in mysterious ways."

What can Laurence say to that? Nothing, if he wants to keep the allegiance of his men. Silence hangs heavy in the frigid air, so I fill the void with my proposal. I describe how we might access the door without rendering the Site unsafe, using Madeline's approach as my secret model, and how we might divide into four teams to provide Site and Relic support while simultaneously excavating.

Archons and Boundary alike voice their willingness to try my idea. Laurence has no choice but to sanction my suggestion, though he gives me a cold glare before he begins to form us into teams. When he doesn't assign Theo to a team immediately—no surprise, as it's been years since Theo's excavated a Site, and I'm guessing he'd rather remain a spectator—I pull him to my side. I'll need an ally in this.

The gambit works. Laurence places us together on a team with eight others, all Boundary Climbers and workers. We start to suit up for the descent into the Site, when he calls out, "Who will excavate the ice packed around the door?"

Strange that he is calling for volunteers. Laurence acts more as dictator out here than leader seeking the loyalty and respect and consensus of his team. Perhaps he's trying to win them back from me. Or perhaps he's breaking from his usual leadership style because the excavation work around the door is the most dangerous? The most susceptible to an avalanche if the support walls collapse?

I'm not certain others will volunteer. I should be the one to place myself at risk, given that this dig design is my suggestion. But more important, I have my own reasons for wanting to be first inside the deck cabin. Before anyone else can Claim it, I throw my hand up in the air. "We will," I call out.

Theo stares at me, a mixture of terror and anger in his eyes. No doubt he's furious that I usurped his senior role by volunteering and terrified at the thought of such a risky excavation after all these years, but I have no choice.

Laurence looks me up and down. His glance holds no mysteries. He's weighing the delight of placing me in a treacherous position with his wariness over the danger.

As he deliberates, I hear a whisper of "braggart" among the Archons. They think I'm trying to uncover the best Relic by entering the *Genesis* first, but they didn't volunteer, did they? Whatever the reason, however I come by it, I need to be the first one through that door.

Laurence renders his verdict. "Archons Eva and Theo, you may have the honor."

XVI.

Julius 11
Year 242, A.H.

Poor Archon Theo. Even with two harnesses strapped together, he barely fits into the climbing apparatus. Although a pair of Boundary workers hold the bulk of his weight by securing his sealskin rope as we lower ourselves into the Site, he's sweating. Out of fear or effort, I don't know.

Side by side, he and I descend into the deep ice hollow. Two Boundary Climbers flank us on ropes, along with another two Climbers in front, scouting out the Site's safety and carrying the heavy load of equipment. There are two more attendants on the ice ledge, awaiting our instructions, in addition to those two holding Theo's line.

I study them carefully, wishing for a glimpse of Lukas's uncle, the white-haired Climber who helped me in the

Testing, or another friend of Lukas's I might recognize. When I last saw him, Lukas promised that his people would be helping my work as the *Angakkuq*—if they could. I'd like to have a true ally down here, one who knows what I'm really doing. But I don't recognize anyone. I'm surrounded, but alone.

When we reach the bottom of the hollow, I motion for some slack in my line. Once I find my footing, I walk around the icy pit, orienting myself. Closing my eyes, I envision Madeline's sketch of the Site. Then I kneel down and run my hands along the surface. Remembering Lukas's teachings about all the different sorts of ice, I notice a few *qopuk*, frozen ice bubbles, trapped in a line deep in the ice floor. I'm guessing it's the line of the door, the one that slammed behind Madeline as the *Genesis* slipped into the ice beneath her and sank into the frozen waters.

I signal to the four Boundary Climbers who accompanied us and etch an outline of the door with my pick. "Here is where we should start."

The door is probably several feet beneath the surface, so it might take the Climbers a few bells—maybe into tomorrow—to reach it. I grab a shovel to start digging, but a Boundary Climber puts his hand on my arm. "We will use the fire, Archon Eva."

I back away as the Climbers pull out fire-wielders from the packs. I watch as their concentrated fire melts the outline of the door I inscribed into the ice. When I step back to give them space, something sharp slices into my calf. I fall to the ground.

What in the Gods cut me? I wince and look around, spying a jagged section of the hull. It juts out of a patch of melting ice. But it seems too low to the ground to have cut my leg. Could someone have done this to me?

The pain grows, and I have to stifle a cry. I can't afford to appear weak; Laurence is looking for any excuse to remove me from this excavation. I sink down and reach over toward a pick lying on a snow mound—as if that explains why I'm on the ground. I surreptitiously lift up my pant leg.

Blood pours down my calf, freezing the tick it hits the air. The wound is several inches long and deep, so deep I can make out the whiteness of bone. I feel like retching. As I stare at the bloody icicles forming on my skin, I realize that I better get some kind of tourniquet on it, the way Lukas showed me.

I slide my hand into a Boundary Climber pack nearby and pull out a length of sealskin rope. Unsheathing my *ulu*, I cut off a small piece of the rope.

Theo approaches me just as I tie off the tourniquet knot and roll down my pant leg. "Don't you want to watch as the Climbers melt the ice?" he asks.

"Of course. Just needed to grab something from my bag," I say, trying to convince myself as much as him. I stand, but I'm unsteady on my feet. My leg feels weak.

"What's wrong, Archon Eva?"

"Nothing. Just a scratch."

"Let me see."

"No, Archon Theo. I appreciate your offer, but I'm fine."

He takes hold of my shoulders and looks me in the eyes. "We need your strength for this dig, Archon Eva. You see that I'm too old and weak to be of much physical help. Without you, we will lose the chance to be first inside the door of the *Genesis*. Don't you want to have that honor?"

He certainly knows how to get to me. "Yes."

"Then let me look at that leg."

There is no choice. I sit down and roll up my pant leg for him. No matter how many *siniks* I serve as an Archon, I will always feel like a Maiden when a man looks at my bare skin.

Panting from the exertion, he lowers himself to the ground to examine it more closely. "By the Gods, how did this happen?"

I shrug, then motion toward the metallic piece of the hull sticking out from a snow mound, because I can't actually speak, or I'll risk throwing up. Now that the blood has stopped dripping from the wound, I glimpse my leg bone once more. I feel nauseated again.

"Hmm," he says, glancing at it and then back at my leg. "No matter. You've staunched the bleeding quite well with that tourniquet; now we've got to sew you up. I just pray to the Gods that your muscles aren't severed." He reaches into a pack around his waist, pulling out a needle and a piece of thread that looks like hair, along with several rare glass jars.

"Before I stitch it, I'm going to put some remedies on it," he murmurs. "These will help clean the wound and speed the healing, but they might sting a little."

My eyes widen at the word, and for a tick I almost forget the pain. Remedies? Did he just say *remedies*? I glance down and see him rub some *pujualuk* into the wound. How in the Gods does Theo know about *pujualuk*?

Almost instantly the sting subsides, replaced by numbness. I only know of this Boundary remedy, derived from a little plant that grows in damp mossy areas, because Lukas had instructed me in its healing properties before the Testing. I wonder if Theo had a Companion long ago who showed him Lex-forbidden Boundary ways as well.

"I'm going to sew the wound up now, so it's best if you look away."

I do, trying to keep my mind fixed on the fact that Theo might actually be more of an ally that I thought. What with violating The Lex in my presence, and with my acceptance, he's managed to turn us into secret accomplices. It's both frightening and thrilling, even more so than the stitchery he's about to perform on my leg. But having sewn up Jasper's wound on the Testing using these medicines and Lex-banned techniques shown to me by Lukas, I know how painful this will be.

Suppressing a scream, I hold my breath. Theo pierces my skin and sews quickly. The numbness fades. I don't think I've ever known such pain. I exhale only when he finishes and then watch as he places upon the wound a thin sheet of bearded seal blubber with the oil removed. Lukas had explained to me how this would act as a bandage.

But how does Theo know?

"This should do it. Let's get you standing so we can see whether the muscle was injured." He struggles to his feet, then pulls me up. At his prodding, I walk a little. The wound hurts, but my leg seems fine.

"Easy," he breathes. "Remember what I've tried to teach you: slow and steady wins the race."

"How can I thank you?" I whisper.

"By keeping secret my use of medicines."

"Of course, Archon Theo. I am in your debt."

"I'm glad that you can be trusted." He glances at me, a knowing smile on his lips. "We all have our secrets, don't we?"

XVII.

Julius 11
Year 242, A.H.

The sun sets over the Frozen Seas, and still the ice does not yield the *Genesis* door. We have no choice but to return to the campsite for the evening. That means that forty-one Archons and Boundary will be trailing in my wake, no doubt snickering at my fruitless efforts. I try my hardest not to limp back to the campsite; I don't want to provide further reason for ridicule.

I am frustrated and embarrassed after all my boasts about the Gods granting me the knowledge of how to unlock the *Genesis*'s secrets. Not to mention weak and hurting. All I want is to burrow into my *iglu* for the night. But protocol requires that I attend the evening meal and nightly meeting; Laurence can even punish me if I don't. After taking my time unloading my packs and delaying

my entry to the last possible tick, I head toward the campfire. I bite my cheek as I mask my limp.

I'm right to be wary. There at the head of the campfire
waits Laurence, a rare smile bright on his face. "So pleased
you've decided to join us, Archon Eva. Finally."

I grab a plate of food and sit in the open spot farthest
from Laurence. But he's not going to leave me alone. Of
course not. He's too eager to relish my failure. "The group
would like to hear what you found in your section of the
dig today."

They know that I didn't find anything. He just wants me
to say it aloud. For the humiliation. "Nothing," I mumble.

"Speak up. We can't hear you."

"Nothing, Archon Laurence," I say louder.

"Nothing, you say. No door to the deck of the *Genesis*?"

"No, Archon Laurence."

"No Relics of any kind?"

"No. Not yet."

Laurence puts his own plate aside, stands, and steps
closer to where I'm sitting, looming over me. "'Yet,'
you say. What makes you think you will be granted a
'yet'? What makes you think that you will be given more
time?"

"That decision is up to you, Archon Laurence."

"That's correct. It will be my choice. And I've been
thinking about how long to let your little proposal proceed before using the bonfires as I suggested earlier. Any
thoughts, Archon Eva?"

Theo gives me a glance across the fire, but doesn't say
anything. I know better than to answer.

Laurence continues. "We will see how you progress. But
never forget that the decision is mine, and you must make

haste. We can't afford to waste a single bell on any of your silly schemes. Summer is coming."

The men nod in agreement. How easily they are swayed. Or is it all fear of their leader? Or continued dislike of a female Archon? Does it even matter at this point?

Since Laurence is done making his point, the conversation drifts. I try to fade into the background by keeping silent. As soon as I'm finished with my food, I leave; protocol only requires that much. I take a longer route to my out-of-the-way *iglu*; I don't want to chance running into an angry Archon en route. Plus I don't want anyone to see my lame walk. Strength is more important now than ever.

When I finally reach the entrance to my *iglu*, I see that someone has already been there.

My belongings are scattered about, some blowing away in the gusty wind. There's no way to replace any of the scant items I brought. Wincing and hobbling, I race to gather what I can, so I don't notice it at first. Then I freeze.

There, pinned with an axe over the entrance, is a message. The blade tacks my spare Archon tunic to the ice, spearing it right through the center of the Triad symbol.

My *iglu* was ransacked for a reason. Someone wants me gone.

XVIII.
Julius 12–17
Year 242, A.H.

Six *siniks* pass before we find it. Six *siniks* where my failure is mocked nightly by Archon Laurence. Six of the longest *siniks* of my life. Six *siniks* until my boasts bear fruit and I taste vindication.

As the rivulets of water drain off, the other teams direct the flow on the sides of the dig to ensure the water freezes safely. While we wait, Theo asks, "How did you know?"

"About the Site?"

"No, Eva, of course not," he snaps. "I watched as you mapped out the Site based on all the documents. I knew you were correct about that. I'm talking about the door. There wasn't a single scrap of paper mentioning a door. So how did you know?"

"The Gods," I answer, giving him the same line I gave Laurence.

"The Gods? Really? Please don't patronize me."

"The truth?"

"Yes."

I think of the possibility that would most horrify Theo, with his love of scholarship and documentation, an answer that would quiet his questioning in its offensiveness. "A hunch."

His jaw drops. "You can't be serious."

"But I am."

"You brought a team of forty-two out here on a hunch? And subjected yourself to Archon Laurence's taunting and mortification on a hunch?"

"No, I was certain of the *Genesis* Site. The proposal that we look for the door instead of using the bonfires was based on a hunch. Perhaps the Gods were responsible," I add.

Before Theo can answer, one of the Climbers calls out to us, and we rush to his side. Crouching down next to him, I see the handle to a door. I glance up at Theo. He shakes his head at me, but a smile curls his lips.

"Thank the Gods," he says. "It looks like you're right, Archon Eva. I can't account for what Archon Laurence would have done to you if you were wrong. Never mind your father."

I smile back and instruct the Climber to melt a few feet more around the door's perimeter. Theo and I stand by and watch, but I can hardly stand it. I'm itching to get down there before anyone else. Especially before Laurence.

The very tick that the door looks clear enough to enter, I reach again for my pick. Lex protocol requires that the most senior Archon on Site give permission to enter, but I don't wait for Laurence to weigh in. I can't risk his certain denial of my request; he'd want the glory for himself. Anyway, didn't Laurence implicitly give me permission to open the door? He assigned my team this task, so he must have expected that if we were successful, we'd be the first to cross the ship's threshold. I think I could make a Lex-based argument on that. At least, that's what I mutter to Theo when he objects.

I wedge my pick into the tiny gap between the door and its frame. I pry the door with all my might, and it opens with a whoosh. Before Laurence truly comprehends what's happening, I gesture to the Boundary workers on the surface to lower us into the room. Just Theo and me. Alone.

Using my *naneq* to light the way, I see only a pitch-black, cavernous room. As I suspected, it's wide open, not ice-locked at all. It seems that when the *Genesis* sank after Madeline's discovery, the deck cabin door slammed tight behind her, sealing shut the cabin as the boat submerged. This means that if the Tech she described is still here, it might be intact. And I just might be able to open it later with Lukas's expertise.

After a few ticks, I'm able to get my bearings. The floor is so slanted beneath us that we'd slide headlong into the opposite wall if we weren't harnessed. There are footsteps in the snow that can only be Madeline's.

I cannot help but gasp. On the tables and wedged on walls, I see it all. The Tech she described. The Tech I'd been hoping to find.

Theo sees it, too.

"Tech," he cries out. His voice cracks. He pulls on his line like a madman, desperate to flee from the room.

I look up at the two Boundary Climbers staring down on us. Unlike Theo, they show no fear. In fact, I imagine they have to hide their snickers. Like me, they understand the truth about Tech. They give me the tiniest of nods, and in that tick, I realize that they know who I am and what I'm here to do. We are on the same side. I feel the comfort of Lukas's arms all the way from the Aerie. I knew he wouldn't have abandoned me.

I also realize that no matter his liberal view of The Lex in the matter of medicines, Theo is otherwise an innocent. He has no comprehension of the truth about Tech or anything else. He believes what all the Aerie people believe, that Tech is evil. That it holds a terrible, dark, and destructive power. He has no clue that these strange objects are just tools, devices. The evil—or the good—only derives from those who wield them.

Would all the Archons be as terrified as Theo is now? Are they all so ignorant? I think of my father, of how he knew the mirror could help me in the Testing. But the mirror wasn't Tech. Is the truth about New North kept to a select few in the Aerie? How much does my father *really* know? Perhaps most of the truth has been lost to time, preserved only in the memories of the Boundary people and in Madeline's journal. For a moment, I wonder if I'm the only keeper of the truth.

But if that's the case, who stabbed my Triad symbol as a warning?

XIX.

Journal of Madeline
Aprilus 24 Year 98, A.H.

J thought J would feel that initial elation forever. For the first few days, J carried around the weight of my secret discovery like a precious talisman. J was delirious at the thought of my finding. When the unearthing began, my Relic revealed itself in satisfying stages, by tick and bell and day. But J remained silent. The calls of "Relic!" from other Testors sounded out, and still J bit my tongue. J felt invincible. J had uncovered part of the Genesis; what could possibly stop me?

When J pried open the door from the Genesis's deck,

I found it packed with Tech. At first I shrugged it off; perhaps the Founders had commandeered an ancient vessel for their holy purpose. But as I dug into the small chamber, the ice felt soft and fell away quickly under the force of my pick. Much too quickly for a hundred-year-old freeze. Still, I held my disquiet at bay and entered with hope. This was hallowed ground, the very place where the Gods visited the first Founders and gave them The Lex. The place from which the Gods led us to the New North.

The sacred place looked ordinary on first glance. The room was lined with simple tables anchored firmly into the metal hull of the ship. The ship's wheel stood in the room's center. A few toppled chairs were still frozen to the floor underfoot. No particular Relic for me to bring to the top, even though a Chronicle of the Genesis itself would be enough for my Archon Laurels.

At that moment, I saw them. Sitting on a tabletop in the back corner were a portable Apple altar and a book bearing a clear symbol of The Lex. I drew closer. The bitten Apple rune on the altar was defaced, almost entirely scratched out.

Was this evidence of the very beginning of mankind's rejection of Apple? Proof of our Founders' acceptance of the true Gods' salvation? My heart started to beat fast, and I clasped my hands for a short prayer.

I dared not touch the Relics, they were so delicate. I drew my lamp over them for a closer look. At that tick,

I noticed something, a fact that had been hovering at the edge of my consciousness but which I had been repressing. The altar and the book were not sealed in ice and bore no signs of long ice-locking. No dissolving of The Lex pages, no rusting of the metallic cover of the altar.

I could no longer ignore my suspicions. Someone had placed these artifacts here recently.

It was the only possible explanation for their fresh condition, for the ease with which I removed the ice and snow from this chamber. The longer I stared at them, the more the Relics reminded me of what mankind called "fiction," the sort long banned by The Lex and the Triad. It was as if they had been placed here by someone who wanted me to tell a particular story to the people of New North. Had Apple himself come here to trick me? At that tick, as I stood at full height in the control room on the deck of the Genesis, I was consumed with a fear I'd never known. The Testing had been aptly named. This was a Test of the gravest kind.

What in the Gods should I do? Who would I be accusing of this awful deed? Only Archons were permitted on the Frozen Shores, and to blame them of tampering with this holy Site would be tantamount to treason. Anyway, what proof did I have, other than my gift for reading the ice and snow? If I wrote a Chronicle that shared my misgivings, I could suffer punishment under The Lex, and so could my family. Banishment to the Boundary lands would be the least of the possible sentences; I had seen people swing from nooses for less. Anyway, what purpose would this sacrifice serve? To undermine The Lex? To mock the Gods? To destroy the New North? But how could J Chronicle what J found?

This had to be a test of my faith and loyalty. J was alone with the Gods. J wished my papa or one of my Teachers or a Basilikon were here. As J hesitated, Father Earth shifted the ground under my feet. J lurched, crashing into a corner of one of the stationary tables. Warmth trickled down my cheek, and touching my glove to it, J realized it was blood. The air filled with a deafening shriek that could only be the Genesis breaking free from her ice casing. Every warning ever issued by every Archon flashed through my mind. Suspended on my sealskin rope, which mercifully J had kept tied around my waist, J swung like a pendulum. As J pulled myself to the surface hand over hand up the rope, trying to block out the awful cracking below, J had no choice but to conclude that this event was a message from the Gods themselves. An answer to my quandary. "Think on The Lex," the Gods seemed to say with each wrench of the ice. The Lex commands that Testors write Chronicles about the Gods' redemption of mankind, not Chronicles that challenge everything we believe.

As J climbed out of the chasm, J made a promise to the Gods in exchange for my life: Jf J survive, J will hew to Your message. J will follow Your commands. J will write a Chronicle about my Relic worthy of The Lex and worthy of mankind's second chance. No matter my misgivings. J inscribe again from memory the words of The Lex:

Mankind is only as sinful as his darkest secrets. For it is in this darkness that the false god Apple worms his way into the hearts and spirits of mankind. Man must close off this opening to darkness. No whispering of confidences may pass, no clandestine writing of private affairs may take place, no secret thoughts may fester. Jf mankind rejects this admonition, he rejects the salvation of the Gods on Earth and beyond. Mankind must shine the light of the Gods into the darkness to secure this, his second—and last— chance at redemption.

—The Lex, 214:78

XX.
Julius 17
Year 242, A.H.

I climb over to Archon Theo and try to calm him. "This is our sacred job as Archons," I murmur. "To drive the evil of Apple from our hearts and minds and excavate this sacred Site. This is the *Genesis*, the blessed ship that delivered some of our Founders here to New North at the command of the Gods. This is where Apple was first defeated. We have nothing to fear here, Archon Theo."

He takes a labored breath. "You're right, Archon Eva. Please forgive me. All this Tech"—he gestures around the room—"just came as such a shock."

I clasp his hand. Even through all our sealskin layers, I can feel him shaking. This is what Tech does to those who don't understand its true nature. This is exactly what the Founders of New North wanted.

"Let's grid the room," I say. I know that this standard task will soothe and occupy him.

"Yes, yes. That's exactly what we should do."

I set him to work mapping out the size and shape of the room's opening and all the objects within its walls. Holding tight to my line, I move around the room. My leg still throbs occasionally with the wound, though Theo's quick administrations might have saved my life. Anyway, there's no reason to mask my pain in front of him.

Plain tables are anchored into the metal hull that Madeline described. The ship's wheel sits right in the center of the room, just as she detailed. The chairs she saw scattered around the room now sit in a heaping pile on the wall opposite the door, no doubt from the shifting of the ship. And the Tech is everywhere.

"You were right to focus on this task, Archon Eva. It's critical that we memorialize this room in the exact state that we found it. This is the *Genesis*, after all." His voice is steady now that he has Lex dictates to follow.

On the table farthest from the floor, wedged in a corner between the table and the wall, I spot some Tech and the early version of The Lex. Exactly as Madeline must have left them. Now it's my turn to control my voice.

"Why don't I focus on this area of the room? It might be a little—" I pause, as if trying to select the proper words. "—challenging for you to access."

He looks across the room and down the steeply pitched floor and nods. No more convincing is necessary. "Yes, that's a good idea."

Clinging to my sealskin rope, I maneuver into a safe spot. I make a show of pulling out my gridding equipment and finding a steady spot to make my recordings. I start by plotting the table and jumble of chairs, and then move onto the Tech heaped against the wall. I am careful to grid everything except the portable Apple altar—laptop, I correct myself—and the book with the Lex emblem on the cover. These are the artifacts that had so troubled Madeline.

Finally I take out my own journal and make a careful sketch of the laptop with its defaced Apple symbol and copy the unfinished Lex pages as best I can. I want to assess for myself the suspicions they raised in Madeline's mind.

Noises begin to echo in the room. A stomping of feet, followed by raised voices. I look up for the Boundary Climbers who are supposed to be at the doorframe, but they've disappeared. Theo and I glance at each other. I think we both know what's happening. Archon Laurence has discovered our entry.

I will not rise to the Site surface empty-handed like Madeline. Her lack of evidence about her findings and suspicions led to her downfall. I won't let that happen to me, even if it makes a thief out of me under The Lex. For the third time.

Anyway, what is The Lex? If it's as flawed as I suspect, if it's a man-made document created to manipulate the New North people, then I don't care if its laws deem me a thief. If it's not, if the Gods truly divined it and They are indeed real, then I think They will forgive me. They will understand that I seek truth above all else.

I only have a few ticks. While Theo's eyes are fixed on the door, I reach for the laptop and The Lex. But the distinctive *kamiks* of Archon Laurence descend on his line lower into the room before I can slide them into my pack. I have no choice but to leave the laptop and The Lex.

"How dare you two enter this room without permission?" he yells, though he need not in this echo chamber.

"My apologies, Archon Laurence," Theo rushes to say. "I understood your group assignments to mean that we had permission to cross the threshold." I suppress a smile as he echoes my very excuse.

"Don't cover for her Lex violations!" Laurence yells even louder. He glares over at me, then back at Theo.

The two men stare at each other. Theo speaks first. "Don't you dare, Laurence."

Laurence turns to face him directly. "What did you call me?"

"I called you Laurence. The name I called my brother for the first forty years of his life. Before he became the second-in-charge of the Archons, and too important to remember his family ties. And honor them as The Lex commands."

My lips part, and for a moment my jaw hangs slack. Brothers? I glance at one, then the other. I guess I see the resemblance despite the years and stones between them. But why is Theo risking so much to help me? Even if Laurence is his brother? *Especially* if Laurence is his brother?

"Don't think that wielding our family connection like a sword will make me back down from this Lex-break, Theo," Laurence fumes. "This isn't your battle."

"Laurence, my battle is to serve the Gods against the darkness, and if that means bending The Lex to do Their will better, I will fight. Archon Eva has led us directly into the heart of the *Genesis*—a blessed Relic we've been seeking since we landed on this island. I will not let you impede her sacred work by some highly technical and overly sanctimonious reading of the protocols of entering Sites!"

I am amazed. Theo is more of an ally than I could've

ever hoped for. And a fiercer opponent than I'd ever suspect. I watch as Laurence slinks away from his incensed
brother, tugs on his line, and rises to the surface. He for-
feits the battle before it even really begins. Or does he have
something else—something worse—planned for me?

"How can I thank you for helping me, Archon Theo?" I
ask once I'm certain Laurence is out of earshot.

"By continuing on with your discoveries, Archon Eva,"
Theo says quietly. "By finishing the work that the Gods
sent you here to do." Even though he's panting from the
heated exchange, he turns his attention back to his gridding.

How could I steal the laptop and The Lex after Theo
took such risks to protect me? No, if discovered, my thiev-
ery would only fuel Laurence's anger against him. I can't
do that to Theo. Or to myself. I will have to find another
way to get these Relics into Lukas's hands.

XXI.

Julius 31
Year 242, A.H.

I throw open the door. Funny, I've lived in this house all my life, and I've never once opened the door for myself. Attendants have always been standing at the ready, eager to serve me, first as the helpless Maiden and then as the newest Archon and recently Betrothed. I never imagined it would be so heavy.

I don't know why I'm surprised the door is unmanned. Why would an Attendant be waiting to assist visitors after the night's final bell? No one knew I'd be returning from the excavation tonight. The only citizens of New North permitted outside of their homes at this time are Triad members. Even Attendants are permitted rest after the final bell, except for the one tending the hearth-fire inside.

After I bid my fellow Archons and Boundary workers

farewell at the Hall, I walked the pitch-black Aerie streets completely alone, sifting through my own thoughts. Of the forty-two that set out on our expedition to the *Genesis*, twenty-four of us returned. Two Archons and fifteen Boundary remained to finish the Site excavations and close it for the season. One poor Boundary Climber won't return at all; Archon Laurence underestimated the swift approach of spring. The melting ice took the Climber down along with it.

As I walked in solitude, I found myself wishing Laurence had fallen with the Climber. I disliked him when we set out, but now I loathe him. His avarice jeopardized us all, and his hatred of me became more apparent as the *siniks* of the dig dragged on. I'd never wished for the Chief title before, but I long for the role now, only to ensure that Laurence doesn't get it. He would turn the sacred office of Chief Archon into a chamber of greed—never mind The Lex's admonitions about the *endless pit that can never be filled*. I wouldn't be surprised if he was the one who speared my tunic to the side of my *iglu*.

The longer I walked, the more I realized that the only thing I'd miss from the dig was spending my *siniks* with Theo. In spite of his ignorance of Tech's true nature, I learned so much from him and his good-natured guidance about the mechanics of an excavation. That, and I'd miss my secret laughs over the sight of him squeezed into his harness. If only we could have been there by ourselves, with our Boundary helpers, then I could have dug deeper into Madeline's hunches about the Tech and The Lex—and the truth lying in the heart of the *Genesis*. But Laurence was too pervasive a presence for that. And I have to admit that he, more than anything, sealed my own reluctance to steal right under Theo's nose.

By a specially prepared sled, Theo and I brought the Tech back to the Hall of Archons. How Theo's hands quaked when we assisted the Boundary workers in loading the sled! I had to restrain from showing my feelings; after all, I'm supposed to believe in Tech's evil power, too. During the *siniks* of our dig, Archon Theo had gotten accustomed to being in the same room as the Tech, but he never got used to touching it. Even through heavily gloved hands.

Such are the misperceptions I must change. I must find a way to examine that Tech.

I close the heavy front door behind me, basking for a moment in the warmth of my family home. It is dead quiet. So quiet that I can hear the rumbles of my father's snoring.

I lower my bags as silently as I can. Instead of heading up to bed like I should, I wander into the dark solar. Even though it's pitch-black, I run my fingers along the familiar surfaces. No torch is necessary for me to recognize the desk where Eamon and I did our Schoolwork every eve. No candlelight is needed to identify the bench where Eamon and I sat for many bells, in punishment meted by our Lady Mother for our wrongdoings. Every object, every corner, tells the history of Eamon and me. A story that's now over, except for my Testing memorial to him.

I could cry, but I'm too tired.

With a sigh, I pass into the kitchen. The hearth-fire glows still; as a symbol of our new life in New North, The Lex commands us to never let its embers die. I walk over to the fire and warm my hands over its low flames. I haven't spent much time in the kitchen since I reached the age of ten and my Nurse Aga left. Where is the larder? I'm starving for real food, not the dried foodstuffs and fire-roasted salmon of the excavation.

Lifting the lid, I find fresh breadrolls and butter. Perfect. I'm just about to bite into a breadroll spread thick with butter when a door slams behind me. I jump, and the bread tumbles out of my hand and onto the floor.

"My apologies, Maiden Eva," an Attendant says. She bends to the floor and retrieves the breadroll. When she looks up at me with tired eyes, I realize that it's Ana. As the youngest Attendant, she's charged with keeping the hearth-fire alive all night. It's a tough task after a full day's service, I'm sure.

"Please don't worry, Ana," I say, and take the breadroll from her hands. Brushing the residue from the well-used kitchen floor off it, I take a big bite.

Ana looks horrified. "Please, let me get you another roll, Maiden Eva. And perhaps some dinner? There're roast fowl and root vegetables left from the dinner your parents had with your Betrothed and his family. I can warm them and serve you in the dining room."

Jasper was here tonight? I feel myself blush a little, thinking of what passed between us the last time he and I were together in this house.

"Don't worry," I tell her. "I just got back from the dig, and after eating on top of a glacier for every meal, this is luxurious."

"At least let me warm the roast fowl for you?"

I'm happy with the breadroll and butter, but Ana is persistent. "All right."

I sit down at the kitchen table and watch as she scampers around, readying the remains of the evening meal. I feel strange being served after serving myself for the *siniks* of my excavation. I also feel safe—truly at ease—for the first time since my *iglu* was ransacked. My thoughts

turn from the warning to Eamon to Lukas and once again
to the task I promised myself I'd fulfill. But how will I
make sense of the Tech hauled back to the Aerie without
Lukas?

I steel myself to ask a question. "Do you remember
Lukas?" Just saying his name aloud instead of keeping it
locked inside my heart and head feels as if I'm violating a
rule. People of the Aerie do not often think of those from
the Boundary unless necessary, let alone mention them.

Ana looks up from the hearth-fire. Hesitating, she says
"Yes."

"I wonder where he is." I purposely don't ask if she
knows of Lukas's location—Boundary or Aerie, and if
Aerie, where. The Lex discourages talk among the Boundary outside their Aeric home, and I don't want Ana to feel
pressured to reveal something she learned in a way forbidden by The Lex. But I do want to communicate that I am
desperate to know.

Ana returns to the hearth-fire and pretends to busy herself with preparing the meal. I can see that's she's buying
time. Seeing if I'll ask again. I stay quiet, praying to whatever Gods actually exist that she'll tell me what she knows.

Keeping her back to me, she fetches a plate from the
shelves lining the kitchen. As she scoops the food from
the pan onto the plate, she finally says, "I heard he's back
in the Aerie."

Staring down at the meal in front of me, I lift my fork
and casually say, "Hmm. I wonder where he was placed. I
hope it's a nice home or a well-kept Keep."

Our eyes lock for a tick. She searches mine, undoubtedly wondering whether this is some Archon trick. I am
wondering, too, whether I can trust her. Who will she tell

that I asked after Lukas? What are my choices? I leap into the silent breach between us. "I miss him."

Ana exhales in visible relief. We both know that it's a far more serious violation of The Lex for a Maiden to express feelings for a Boundary than it is for a Boundary Attendant to share gossip. I've earned her trust. "Me, too," she says. "I've heard he is serving at the Clothing Keep."

The Clothing Keep. It seems an odd choice for a Boundary as well trained as Lukas. Only manual labor takes place there, not the skilled climbing and hunting and dog-sledding for which he is known. Still, I've found him, and now I must manufacture a way to see him even though he explicitly forbade it. He is my only hope in unlocking the secrets I unearthed in the *Genesis*.

XXII.

Augustus 1
Year 242, A.H.

"What a surprise, darling!" my mother exclaims when I enter the dining room. "Why didn't you let us know you were coming home?"

My parents rise to embrace me, and my father says, "My most recent reports from Archon Laurence were that the excavation was still underway."

Pulling back a little, I explain, "Archon Laurence is still at the Site, finishing up the dig."

"Good. I'm looking forward to getting the full report." Father glances over at Mother and says circumspectly, "It's such an important dig."

"Yes, it is," I say. I am just as cautious. "I'm certain they'll close the Site within the week. They must. Archon Theo says it's very close to the full summer thaw."

"Archon Theo?"

Surely Father knows that Archon Theo accompanied us on the excavation. The Chief oversees all. "Yes, Father. I thought you held him in esteem."

"I do. I'm just astonished that a man of his years and stature would be so close to the Site as to report on its stability. I assumed he would serve in an advisory capacity."

"Well, he was. He was in the dig Site alongside me."

My father gives me his intense Chief Archon look. "Was that Archon Laurence's direction?"

"I don't know, Father. It's not for me to challenge the decisions of Archon Laurence. I took a vow of *pareo*, remember?"

He raises his voice. "Don't lecture me on *pareo*, Eva. Is there something more that you should tell me?" My father rarely shows any sign of temper; the news of Theo's role at the dig must disturb him. "There is a tremendous amount at stake on this dig. Surely you understand that."

There is indeed, but I've said enough. Enough to make my father ask questions, but hopefully not enough to embroil me in a full confession. I want my father to learn the details of Laurence's overreaching and dangerous risks from someone other than me. The Boundary Climber's death must be reported, and Laurence must be held accountable, but making that happen is not my duty. Too much is at stake, as my father said himself.

Glancing over at my mother, I play the Archon, bristling at the talk of work in the presence of Ladies. I say, "Perhaps we should speak of something more appropriate over breakfast."

My mother's face lights up. She loves it when I act the Maiden—or Maidenly Archon, anyway. "Excellent suggestion, Eva. No more Archon talk, Jon. Perhaps some talk of the Union?"

My father doesn't look as pleased; I can see questions and anger simmering beneath his controlled surface. But he acquiesces and gestures for us to sit. "As you wish."

We take our usual seats, and for a tick it seems as though no time has passed at all. We talk of Union plans, Aerie gossip, and the warming weather. We are simply a Maiden and her parents, and we act as if we have never suffered strife or heartache. But then Eamon's empty chair stares back at me, and I realize that we are all just playing roles.

My parents deserve some happiness, however fleeting, so I paint on a Maidenly smile and ask for the herbal tisane. As my mother passes it to me across the elegantly set breakfast table, she smiles. Just as I'm about to congratulate myself for giving her some momentary pleasure, she says, "Have you forgotten something, Eva?"

I look at my plate to see if I've used the wrong utensil or forgotten to lay my napkin in my lap. Too many *siniks* beyond the Ring will make one forget the niceties of Aerie life. Everything looks in order. "I don't think so, Mother."

"It is Basilika Day, Eva. We will leave shortly."

I glance down at my clothes. I'm wearing my Archon black. I've completely lost track of the days of the week. No surprise. On the dig, we only observed Basilika Day— the Lex-ordered day of worship, reflection, and rest—by way of an extra prayer. Otherwise, it was Archon business as usual.

I jump up. "I will change into one of my gowns."

As I bound up the stairs, my mother calls, "Don't forget your hair, Eva."

My hair. I slept in my Boundary-style fishtail plaits,

an updo unbefitting a Maiden on her way to the Basilika. How the Maidens and Ladies of the Aerie would whisper. I can't afford any more attention than I've already garnered. I'll have to bathe and restyle.

As I run up the stairs, I call for my Companion. "Katja!" I'll need her assistance to make it in time. Even as I believe myself to be a strong, self-sufficient Archon, capable of surviving alone beyond the Ring, I quickly fall back into the ways of a Maiden. I wish switching back and forth was as easy as changing my clothes.

Katja races into my bedroom to heat the water for my bath. After she's filled the tub and lit the fire underneath, she opens my wardrobe to ready a gown. She selects a brown dress, suitable enough for the Basilika with its somber shade but flattering enough for the Aerie crowd with an emerald-green trim that my mother says brings out the red of my hair and the greenish hue of my eyes. I nod my approval as I strip off my Archon uniform and wait for the bath to fully warm.

Waiting. How much of a Maiden's time is spent waiting. Time stands still for the keepers of the hearth while their Gallants are out at their callings. This was almost my lot.

XXIII.

Augustus 1
Year 242, A.H.

We hear the chanting of the Basilikons before we reach the doors. My mother flashes me a stern look, but she needn't. I know we are late. I also know the unprecedented tardiness is my fault. It took longer than I'd hoped to scrub the Archon residue off to reveal the Maidenly skin and hair underneath.

The guards betray no expression as they open the ice-doors to the Basilika. Arms linked with my parents, we walk down the aisle. Although I have walked down this aisle several times since the Chief Basilikon performed the Betrothal ceremony for me and Jasper, I haven't felt so many eyes on me since that day. I feel as though I'm reliving the ritual—only without my Betrothed.

Jasper. He must be here. Only illness or duty would keep him from the Basilika on Basilika Day.

After we settle into our designated second-row bench, I glance to my right to see if he's in his usual seat. Jasper's family is accorded a bench level with our own, largely due to the Chief Lexor ranking of his uncle Ian. I don't have to hunt for him. There he is, so handsome in his fur cloak and his blond hair freshly brushed. He catches me, and stares right back, a glowing smile breaking over his face.

I blush and look down. The Lex doesn't prohibit his display of affection, but the boldness and the directness is unusual for the Basilika. I glance over at my mother and father, expecting stern glances, but I observe them exchanging smiles. They're delighted with Jasper's apparent affection. And my Maidenly blushing, no doubt.

The Chief Basilikon calls us to prayer. I find it hard to concentrate. Between Jasper's stares and my internal debate about how to contact Lukas, the Gods aren't foremost in my thoughts. Perhaps They won't be offended. If They even exist, that is.

Thankfully, the Chief Basilikon performs a standard service—no postscript or sermons—and I'm able to make the Lex-required responses without much thinking. Before I know it, we're chanting the final prayer together. When the service ends and the Aerie folk begin to mingle, Jasper strides directly over to me.

"Welcome home," he says and takes my hand in his.

I shiver a little. His touch reminds me of our parting, and I feel myself blush again. How can I feel this way around him but still long for the sight of Lukas? Neither emotion is particularly Maidenly, and together, they are the very opposite.

"It's good to be home," I answer.

"I've missed you."

I smile back at him. "And I you."

"Why didn't you send word that you were returning? I would have waited for you at your home."

"I didn't know myself until yesterday. There wasn't time to send a hawk."

"You returned from the Frozen Shores to the Aerie in one day?" His face shows his disbelief. After the long trek that we took to the Frozen Shores as Testors, a journey that took weeks and inflicted much misery and suffering, it is hard to accept that the travel could be so short. Particularly with what it means about our leaders.

"Yes. It is as we thought," I answer, trying to hint at my meaning. I'm eager to share my observations with him. To see if he is indeed on my side.

He grasps at clarity. "Truly, it only—"

Jasper's mother interrupts. "Eva, darling, we are so glad to see you safely home."

Our parents engage us in their chatter. As Jasper and our fathers talk of his Forge preparations, our mothers pick up a conversation about my Union gown that seems to have started on an earlier day. My mother has showed me the lavish dress, and it appears that she's spent much of my time away on its embroidery. Probably with Jasper's mother at her side.

An idea occurs to me. "Mother, do you think that they would open the Clothing Keep for us today?"

She laughs, puzzled. "Why on His Earth would you need to visit the Clothing Keep today? Or any day, for that matter."

"Well, you know that I adore that lovely light blue you chose for the Betrothal Gown?"

"Yes, dear." Her voice is up to its Lady-pitch, because she senses I'm up to something. "Blue is the only suitable shade for a Union ceremony. The symbol of man and woman joining together just as mankind joined together with the will of the Gods, the God of the Earth in particular: *Blue of the sky, blue of the seas, blue of His Earth.*" She quotes The Lex for Maidens.

"The color is exquisite," Jasper's mother chimes in.

"Oh, the color is beautiful," I agree, and I even mean it. "I'd just been hoping to accent it with a vivid blue. You know, like the rich waves of the Frozen Seas."

My mother studies me. "I've never seen the Frozen Seas, Eva," she says wistfully. How sad to think that she lives here on this island surrounded by nothing else but water, and yet she's never laid eyes on the ocean. Again I am conscious of how strange I must seem to these Ladies, to have witnessed a sight previously reserved for men. And only a select few men at that.

"Nor have I. Can you describe it?" Jasper's mother looks so eager that I almost feel bad for my deceit.

"It is entrancing yet ever-changing. At one tick, like the bright blue of the early spring night sky, and at the very next tick, like the blueberries they grow in the Ark for the Aurora festival."

"The seas contains that many shades of blue?"

"Yes. More."

The Ladies exchange a glance. My mother asks, "You have your heart set on this, my dear?"

"I do."

The Ladies nod at each other. They approve of my

suggestion and want to encourage my Maidenly interest in the Union gown. Up until now, I've been so focused on my Archon work.

"Must it be today?" my mother asks. "It's Basilika Day."

"I work as an Archon on every other day."

"True. But surely I could choose the thread while you are working."

"But that is my point, Mother. How would you know which shade to choose? You've never seen the Frozen Seas."

After so many years with my strong-willed father, my mother knows when she has lost an argument. Although she rarely wields her power for self-serving reasons, she relents. "I'll send word to the Clothing Keep." She issues an instruction to the Attendant who's been following along on our walk.

I know that no one will dare deny Lady Margret, wife of the Chief Archon. Perhaps today I will see Lukas.

XXIV.
Augustus 1
Year 242, A.H.

As we amble from the Basilika to the Clothing Keep, the narrow streets of the Aerie bustle with other Basilika Day strollers. Jasper's mother and mine pay due respect to those we pass, pausing to nod at a fellow Lady or say a brief word to a Keeper's wife, but their chatter focuses on my Union ceremony dress. For good reason, Ladies praise my mother's handiwork as the finest in the Aerie, and the two women linger over decisions about where my mother should place a delicate snowflake design or inlay a rare crystal. I try not to let their excitement poison me with guilt over yet another deception.

Jasper walks beside me in silence, pretending to listen to our fathers' talk of the harvest, but we cannot be alone. He knows this, too. My consideration of the Union garb is all too rare, and my father doesn't want to waste a tick of this time stolen from my Archon duties.

With a shrug of apology, Jasper allows himself to be led away by my father to a group of Lords and Gentlemen talking in the Aerie town square. It's just as well. We will arrive at the Clothing Keep soon, and it is no place for a Gallant.

I smile sadly to myself. It's funny how even I slip back into my old role and way of thinking. Once I shed my Archon clothes, that part of me is put aside, too.

Glancing up again to give Jasper a farewell wave, I notice that a large crowd has gathered in the town square. A much larger crowd than called for by the usual Basilika Day mingling. What is happening? I signal to my mother to wait a tick, and while she idles patiently in the street with Jasper's mother, I step into the square.

There on the center dais, I see the reason for the crowd. There on the platform stands the gallows. Empty.

Strange. I'm certain that the gallows wasn't there when I passed by the town square last evening. After I returned to my family home in the dead of night, someone must have been hard at work erecting the wooden scaffolding necessary for the horrific public punishment of hanging.

Why was the gallows built so quickly? It's rare for a hanging to take place on Basilika Day; only the most heinous of crimes, those in most need of urgent punishment, are permitted on this day. What crime could have necessitated this?

My stomach churns at a nauseating thought. Could the timing of the gallows be related to our return from the *Genesis* Site?

"Eva," my mother calls from the street.

I ignore her, mesmerized by what's happening on the

dais. The Ring-Guards lead a stumbling man up its stairs. A rough-hewn bag covers his face, so I cannot tell his identity. Still, I can see from his clothes that he is Boundary. My pulse quickens. By the Gods, I pray it isn't Lukas. Could someone have found out about our visits and communications? Wouldn't I have been told, as I'd be complicit?

"Eva!" she calls again. This time, her voice bears no Lady-quality. But I cannot turn away no matter what price I'll pay with her anger. I must find out the criminal's identity and Lex-violation.

A Herald steps onto the dais. "People of New North, hear this!"

A hush falls over the assemblage. People crane their necks and stand on their tiptoes for a glimpse at the condemned.

"A terrible crime has been committed against the Aerie!" the Herald continues. His rich voice seethes with contempt. "This Boundary"—he practically spits the word—"was given a gift. He was allowed to rise far above his birth and bequeathed a precious task by the Archons themselves. One entrusted with a sacred duty on a sacred Archon Site. A fact that makes his Lex-breaking all the worse."

I stop breathing. This must relate to the *Genesis* Site. But how? I feel a quick flood of relief that this poor soul can't be Lukas, but am just as quickly sickened by the notion that Archon Laurence might have orchestrated the hanging.

"This Boundary was charged with returning to the Aerie priceless Relics found on an excavation only days ago. Instead of securing all these Relics within the safety of the Hall of Archons, the Ring-Guards found one of those precious Relics in his bag as he made the Passage back out into the Boundary Lands."

The crowd gasps. Shouts of "Thief!" echo from the more zealous Aerie. Other than outright murder, The Lex contains no greater offense. But I find the accusation almost impossible to believe. The Boundary are gifted at many things, particularly at concealment from the Aerie. If this Boundary indeed took an item from the Site, no Ring-Guard would have found it. This must be Laurence's doing.

More outraged shouts ring out from the throngs of Aerie. Some call out for the criminal's immediate death. Other cry out for justice, which is basically the same thing. One lone, loud voice screams, "What is the Relic that he stole?"

Prepared for this query, the Herald reaches into a sack and steps forward. He thrusts out over the crowd a single object. The hooting and jeers grow even louder—uncertain of the nature of the Relic but certain of the Boundary's guilt.

They might not know what the Relic is, but I sure do. It is a boot. A hard, inflexible climbing boot from the pre-Healing days. The sort we used for training in the Hall of Archons. The sort of which we saw no evidence at the *Genesis* Site. The useless sort that no right-minded Boundary person would ever steal. As I watch the Guards wrap the noose around the Boundary man's neck, it hits me. I realize precisely what this hanging is. A message from Laurence to me to stay out of his way. And in that sudden moment, I know with dread certainty that he was the one who ransacked my *iglu* and left the message for me back at the *Genesis* Site as well.

XXV.

Augustus 1
Year 242, A.H.

I am shaken by what Archon Laurence has wrought. I can barely maintain my composure as I continue to stroll toward the Clothing Keep with my mother and Lady Charlotte. Thank the Gods they're so wrapped up in the gown that they barely take notice of me. I'm not even sure if they noticed the hanging. Besides, deriving pleasure from such gruesome justice is not behavior befitting a Lady or Maiden.

The Clothing Keeper stands at the threshold. As he steps aside at the open door, he smiles broadly, proud to display his finest fabrics and threads. Only the best of his wares are available to a Lady of such high rank. While I'm certain that he'd rather be spending his one day of rest doing something else, I know that he's eager to please the

uncompromising Lady Margret. Her word is nearly tantamount to The Lex in all things concerning the hearth and
home.

Despite the overcast day, the Keep interior is bright. The
Keeper has arranged for nearly a dozen torches to be lit
around the room. The front table is already laid out with
many threads in varying shades of blue. Someone was hard
at work in the ticks between our summoning and our walk
from the Basilika. But the Keeper is alone. Where are the
Attendants? I came here for Lukas, after all, not to improve
my Betrothal gown.

"My Ladies." The Clothing Keeper bows and gestures
toward the threads.

We approach the table. The array is sumptuous, and I
cannot keep from fingering the silken threads. The Keeper
is reputed to have unparalleled skill with the dye, and
his reputation is warranted. The range of blues is enormous yet subtle. I see sky blue, azure, cobalt, aquamarine,
navy—more colors than I have names for.

"They are lovely," I say.

"Beautiful," Jasper's mother echoes.

"Is there one in particular that catches your fancy,
Maid—" The Keeper isn't certain how to address me.
"Arch—"

My mother interrupts, ever happy to display her knowledge of Lex protocol. "Eva is here as a Betrothed today, so
it's best to address her as Maiden."

"They are truly exquisite, but . . ." I force my voice to be
slow and hesitant.

"But what, Maiden Eva? I am here to serve you."

"Do you have any others?"

"Any others? Eva, I've never seen so many blues. Not

even in the midwinter night sky." My mother punctuates her remarks with an embarrassed chuckle. Her voice is back up to its Lady-pitch; it always rises this way when she's making up for my behavioral lapses. She probably doesn't want Jasper's mother to think I'll be a persnickety wife.

"Maybe a thread dyed with a berry grown elsewhere? Beyond the Ring? Or perhaps in the Boundary lands?" I offer.

"The Ark grows the finest berries in New North, Maiden Eva. The Lex tells us so. And I only use Ark berries." The Keeper's smile falters for an instant, unsure of why he's being forced to defend his practices. I can't blame him.

"Hmm. There is a certain blue that I've seen in the glaciers bordering the Frozen Seas, a color that makes brilliant the waters. I would love to see its hue on my Union gown. Perhaps you have something like it here?"

The Keeper glances at the Ladies. "I'm not familiar with that shade, Maiden Eva. I have never been beyond the Ring."

"Ah," I say, as if that explains the absence of this particular thread. "Might I see your dye shop?"

He laughs a little at my suggestion. I'm guessing he's wondering if it's a joke, as I doubt any Lady or Maiden has ever asked to set foot in the back of his Keep. "My dye shop. Whatever for, Maiden Eva?"

"Perhaps if I look at your dyes, I might be able to find that exact shade. Or guide you to combine two dyes that might approximate the color on which I have my heart set." I glance at him. "I've seen this blue beyond the Ring."

The Keeper bows low. It is the bow of a Keeper to an Archon, not the bow of a Keeper to a Maiden. In a tick our roles have changed.

"Ladies?" He gestures for us all to follow him into the Keep.

My mother's eyes are ice as they meet mine for an instant. Then she turns to the Keeper and titters, "Oh, no, Keeper. We couldn't possibly. That wouldn't be a fitting place for us."

The Keeper is no longer smiling. Now he just appears confused. Again I can't blame him. Nobody is sure of the next move. If the interior of the Clothing Keep is unsuitable for my mother, how can he possibly lead her Maiden daughter back there unescorted? The new rules concerning the Maiden-Archon Eva are confounding.

My mother sighs. "Keeper, you have my permission to take Maiden Eva to the back." She squares her shoulders. "After all, she has seen *many* things that most of us have not—Lady and Lord alike. Like the Frozen Seas."

I smile at my mother. Her flash of anger has melted. The pride there is real. All at once, my throat tightens, and tears sting the corner of my eyes. I've never, ever witnessed her so proud of me. I square my shoulders right back. "I'm ready."

As the Keeper leads me to the farther reaches of the Keep, I note a distinct change in the craftsmanship of the interior. Instead of the heavily polished stone and intricately carved wood found in the Keep's public room, this area, typically seen only by assistant Keepers and Attendants, is made of ice, rough-hewn rock, and timber only when necessary. No adornment here.

No Attendants, either. Where is everyone? True, it is Basilika Day, but someone helped the Keeper open the shop and set up the display of threads.

We work our way farther into the warren of workrooms,

at last entering the area where the thread is dyed. Finally I see an Attendant.

The Attendant's back faces me, as he's busy with a pestle and mortar, crushing buckthorn berries to make a brilliant green shade. I can only see his hands. They are strong and muscular with calluses on every knuckle, and a distinctive scar that comes only from the lightning-fast slide of a sealskin rope across the palm. They are not the hands of a Clothing Keep Attendant but a Climber.

My heart soars. I've found him.

XXVI.

Augustus 1
Year 242, A.H.

I lie awake in the darkness, waiting for the house to quiet. My parents went to bed after the evening meal, but it wasn't until about a half bell ago that I heard the gentle rumbles of my father's snoring. Still, I had to wait; the scurrying sounds of the Attendants finishing their nightly tasks continued until about a quarter bell ago. Only then could I consider my next steps.

I tell myself that I can rise within fifteen ticks. That should be long enough for the whole household to deepen their sleep such that my creeping to the turret won't awaken them. I'm so nervous—about getting caught or seeing Lukas, I'm not sure which—that I can hardly stay still under the covers. That, and the fact that I'm wearing my full Archon uniform under the bedcovers and am boiling hot.

In an effort to still my mind and body, I recall that moment earlier today at the Clothing Keep when Lukas turned and realized I was standing behind him.

His dark brown eyes widened in shock. For an instant his lips formed that wide, rare smile of his. His lips parted as he began to offer greetings before he recollected where we were and who we were meant to be. Then he snapped his mouth shut. And in the next instant, his brow furrowed in anger. He'd made me promise to stay away, to allow him to find me. Still, I wanted to hug him; so fearful I had been for that tick when I thought it might be him on the gallows.

The Keeper ignored Lukas, and I followed his lead. A Maiden of the Aerie would not be expected to recognize an Attendant in any event; eyebrows would be raised if I greeted a Boundary worker unprompted. I pretended to hang on the Keeper's every word as he led me past the row of blue dyes, carefully stored in ice bowls. As I did, I brushed up against Lukas's arm, slowing his rhythmic pestle motions.

Standing on my tiptoes, I examined each ice bowl. "These are exquisite, Keeper. Truly."

"Thank you, Maiden Eva."

I returned to the two shades nearest Lukas. Drawing close enough to him that I could hear his breathing, I whispered in my lowest voice, "Tonight I will come."

Before Lukas could react, I summoned the Keeper. "Here. If we combine these two shades, I think we will come close to the brilliant blue of the Frozen Shore's glacial waters."

"Maiden Eva, I will make the most beautiful blue thread for your Union gown that the Aerie has ever seen."

The Keeper offered his hand to guide me back to the

Ladies. I wanted to look back at Lukas one last time, but I couldn't bear to see the expression on his face at the mention of my Union day. I took the Keeper's outstretched hand and returned to the Ladies.

Now, lying here alone and thinking of Lukas, my stomach churns. I know he's furious with me for breaking my oath. But I had no choice; our window to examine the Tech is too small. We must study it before it is moved into some antechamber I can't access. Or worse, either intentionally or ignorantly altered.

I'm sure Lukas will understand. He must. Once he understands that we've found the Tech from the original Founders' ship, the *Genesis*. The very same Tech that raised so many questions for Madeline about the creation of The Lex and the founding of New North. Questions undoubtedly important for Lukas's precious *Angakkuq*.

I slide off the covers and pad onto the floor. My *kamiks* are silent, but my floorboards are not. They creak like the ravens of spring. I walk in the heel-toe manner Lukas taught me for hunting, and the creaking stops. Before anyone is the wiser, I'm down the hallway and onto the turret. I breathe hard, making a cloud in the air before me. Scanning the landscape brightened slightly by the half-moon, I see no one. Not a single Ring-Guard making his rounds or a lone Aerie guard patrolling the Aerie lanes. This is my moment.

I drive my ice screw into a crevice between the stones of the turret. My line drops to the ground a hundred feet below with a satisfying thud. Positioning myself on the rim of the turret, my back to the ground, I slide down the sealskin rope, leave the safety of my home, and pass into the darkness, just like that fateful night I entered the Boundary.

XXVII.
Augustus 1
Year 242, A.H.

It's strange how much power and liberty I had as an Archon beyond the Ring. Even with the incorrigible Archon Laurence in charge, I had the freedom to work at the time and in the manner I saw fit. But once I made the Passage back under the Gate and into the Aerie, the rigid rules of The Lex clamped down on me again, whether I'm Maiden or Archon. Now I am committing almost too many crimes to name. Hurrying across the Aerie town square to speak to a Boundary worker at the Clothing Keep becomes a matter of life or death. The Laurels and a Union. Or the gallows.

My heart pounds as I dart from one familiar doorway to another, ever watchful for movement in the moon shadows or the crunch of snow indicating a Guard's step. The distance is short but seems endless as I creep toward the Clothing Keep. Once there, it's so pitch-black that I find it difficult to locate the back entrance, the one I'm guessing is closer to Lukas's quarters.

But I don't have far to search. Lukas is waiting for me in the arched doorway. And as suspected, he's furious. "You shouldn't be here, Eva." His hiss would surely be a holler if he could risk the volume.

"It's nice to see you, too, Lukas." I understand his anger, but now that I'm here safely, there's no sense frittering away our time on rage.

"You promised me you would not come. You know how important you are—how I do everything I can to protect you. Why would you put yourself in danger like this?"

"Lukas, I had to find you. We found some things on the dig that only you can help me with."

He shook his head. "It's not worth risking your safety, Eva."

"Lukas, I don't think we have the luxury of time. Besides, nobody saw me."

"Eva, don't be naive. We don't know who might be watching."

"You're being paranoid. I might be the first Maiden Archon, but I'm not all that interesting to the Aerie people except as an example to hold up to their daughters of a willful, non-Lexful Maiden."

I've made him really angry. "Paranoid? I suppose that it's paranoia that killed your brother. Have you forgotten what happened to Eamon?"

Now it's my turn to fume. "How dare you! You know better than anyone that Eamon haunts my every thought and action. He is the reason I became an Archon, and he's the reason I risk my life every day to find out the truth."

Lukas deflates and reaches for my hand. "I'm sorry. I

should never have said that. I just don't think I could bear losing you after what happened to Eamon."

My anger disappears, too. I clasp his callused fingers in mine. "I know. But I'm here now. Why waste what little time we have together fighting? Let's use the bells we have to get some answers."

He nods, but won't meet my eyes. I hear such worry in his voice and fear he must know more than he's saying. Maybe a threat more specific than "we don't know who might be watching." But I also know Lukas well enough to know that he won't tell me no matter how hard I press.

"How is your leg?" he asks.

"My leg?" Instinctively I reach down to rub it. "How do you know about that? Some of the Climbers told you, yes? I knew they'd been sent—"

"No, no," he interrupts gently. "I heard about your wound from the Attendants in your home. This time I couldn't arrange for anyone to be out there with you. Certainly not like those I had on your Testing dig."

I straightened, confused. Had those sympathetic nods and glances I'd received been unprovoked? Or had I imagined them in my longing for Lukas? In my longing for safety? Most of all, however, I am shocked about this latest revelation. "You had others in place during the Testing besides your uncle?"

"Quite a few."

A troubling thought occurs to me. "Did you arrange for me to win the Testing?"

Lukas stares at me. "No, Eva. Not at all. You are so important to all of us that we wanted to make sure you were safe. But the victory was yours alone. No one but you could have written that Chronicle. Believe me."

I try to believe as he's so often said before, but I wonder. I decide to squirrel away my questions and concerns and focus on what we might accomplish tonight. "Come on, Lukas. There's some Tech I really need your help to analyze. Tech that came from the *Genesis*."

His eyes continue to hold mine. And now, instead of anger or concern or withholding, all I see in their black depths is excitement. "The *Genesis*?"

"The very one," I answer with a smile.

XXVIII.

Augustus 1
Year 242, A.H.

To make it safely to the outer walls of the Hall of Archons, I need only to follow in Lukas's footsteps. Or so I tell myself. But it's no easy task. His step is so light, and his senses so alert, it's like following a hunting wolf. Still, somehow I manage, even when the Ring-Guards pass overhead.

Once we reach the impenetrable ice-fortress, though, our roles reverse. Now Lukas must rely on me. No matter how developed his senses and skills, the labyrinthine inner layout of the Hall combined with the absence of any exterior openings—save the immense front doors—make the Hall impossible to navigate. We are entirely reliant on my mental mapping and my knowledge of the Yard.

I smile to myself. A small part of me loves that the teacher is becoming the student. Even if it's just for the night.

Lukas glances over at me, the question of how on His Earth we'll enter clear on his face. I motion for him to throw a line over the lip of the exterior wall. He stares at me in disbelief, and I whisper that word he's said to me countless times: "Believe."

He really has no choice but to nod in begrudging agreement. Pulling out his *atlatl*, he shoots a line toward the frigid night sky. We can't see it landing, but it must have sunk deep into the ice on his first shot, because the line is firm when we tug. We strap on our bear-claw boots and begin to climb.

Compared to other ascents we've practiced together, or those I undertook solo beyond the Ring, the distance is small. But the height makes the climb seem deceptively easy. The Archons had prepared for this potential breach of their fortress. The wall is slicker than any either Lukas or I have ever encountered. The Guards must water it each day and let it ice over each night to make it so slippery.

Footholds and handhelds are near impossible. Lukas keeps sliding back down onto me—I had assumed the lower position, as usual in our training—and I keep slipping back down the wall to the ground. We start and restart, ever mindful of the time and the Ring-Guards' schedule, and the going is rougher than any I've experienced, even during the Testing over a bottomless crevasse.

Lukas pulls out a small device. It almost looks like the rakes used in the Ark to cultivate and tend the growing plants. He runs it up and down the wall as we go, roughening the texture. Anywhere else, on any other type of climb, this action would be absolutely prohibited. Loose ice is the death knell of the climber. Unfortunately, we have no choice. The wall is still slick, and we still slide into each other, but now we can make progress. When we finally make it to the top, Lukas and I reel in all evidence of our climb. Except the rake marks, that is.

Now I take over. In the days since we returned from the dig, I've mapped out the safest route to the Yard. I know that there might be traps of which I'm unaware, but I can't think of that as I lead Lukas. There is no point fearing what I don't know.

We traipse over surfaces that act as ceilings for the Conservation Chamber, the main Hall, the Refectory, even the Vault. I try to imitate Lukas's silent, padded step, all the while praying to whatever Gods are out there that the Guards within the Hall hear nothing. I see the edge of the Wall bordering the Yard and turn back to Lukas with a smile.

Just in time to see him fall through the icy surface into the chamber below.

If I hadn't seen him plummet, I would not have believed it. His drop was so quiet—no sound of ice shattering or cracking—that it must have been a trap of thin ice set by the Archons for an intruder. I race to the opening to see his dark shape lying on the floor below. I want to call out to see if he's all right, but I can't. Our only chance of survival is silence.

Instead of dropping the line over the wall bordering the Yard, I drop it just inside that same wall, near where he landed. I try to follow all of Lukas's instructions, but I'm so eager to reach him that I rush. I slide down the line faster than intended and land with a thud.

By this time, Lukas is struggling to stand. I hurry to his side. "Are you hurt?" I whisper.

He brushes me away. "No, I'm fine." Glancing around, he asks, "Does this mess us up?"

No Guards are in sight. I've been down here before; we're in a hallway that leads to the Conservation Chamber. I shake my head. "We're okay. Let's go."

After gathering up our gear, we pad down the hall. I take the lead. I'm following a map that exists only in my mind, and I'm doing it blind. But I get it right. After a few long ticks of slinking around, we stand at the entryway to the Conservation Chamber, precisely as I'd hoped. Ducking into the room, I dare to light my *naneq*. Bringing Lukas all this way won't mean much if he can't see the artifacts.

The silvery Tech glitters in the soft glow like gems. I turn to witness Lukas's reaction.

His eyes are wide. "All this came from the *Genesis*?"

"I brought it here from the deck of the ship myself."

"*All* this Tech?"

"All of it."

Lukas starts laughing. It's a low, guttural sound that I've never heard before. It sounds as if it's coming from another person, not this serious and intense boy I've known my whole life. Then he lifts me up under my arms and twirls me around the room.

XXIX.

Augustus 1
Year 242, A.H.

Elation subsides and industry sets in. Lukas sets me to work setting up a strange light source that he's brought with him. Using words from before the Healing that I only vaguely understand, Lukas tells me that in order to "start" the Tech, we need to "charge" them. Since we can't give the Relics the power from Her Sun they usually require, Lukas has rigged up a substitute. But we won't be certain of its efficacy until we see the Tech's telltale flickering blue light.

As we wait, Lukas examines the Tech that's not being "charged"; we can only attempt to power up two of the Relics at a time. I update him on my findings beyond the Ring: Madeline's journal entries, the scratched-out Apple surface on the laptop, the proximity of the so-called first Lex to that Tech, and Madeline's suspicions. The very moment he acknowledges that I was right to bring him here—a huge victory, though I try not to gloat—the room fills with a familiar bluish light.

The Tech is on. Lukas's contraption works.

"Please start with the damaged one," I implore him. Even if we never make it out of the Hall safely, I've got to see this one Relic's secrets with my own eyes. I owe it to Madeline.

Lukas nods, then starts tapping away at the squares with letters inscribed upon them. He's told me before to call them "keys," but the word feels awkward on my tongue and in my mind. The squares don't look like any key I've ever seen. I can't make sense of what's appearing on the face of this Relic—what I used to think of as the diptych altar to the false God Apple—that I now know to call a "screen." What was once sacred has become profane.

I draw closer as Lukas's fingers clatter furiously. Row after row of numbers appears. Lukas seems mesmerized by them, but they're nonsensical to me. Why is he spending so much time on this? We should be poring over the Tech for more critical information about the beginning of New North, the Founders, the *Genesis*, anything along the lines of Madeline's suspicions. The Archon Guards are prowling. This strikes me as a waste of precious time; our luck is bound to run out.

But in a few ticks, I begin to see what he finds so fascinating.

The numbers are linked to various categories. And while the numbers don't mean much to me, the categories certainly do. They are a list of the items on board the *Genesis*, and the numbers indicate the quantities of those items that the *Genesis* carried. The document is entitled "Manifest."

Interesting that the *Genesis* was fully loaded with nearly everything necessary to sustain life. The hull contained seeds of every sort; multiple pairs of food-producing animals like cows, goats, chickens, and sheep; soil samples; water purification systems; fuel and energy sources; building materials; tools; bountiful quantities of wool, threads, and furs; basic hunting and fishing equipment; climbing gear; compasses and Arctic maps; and countless things I've never heard of.

How would the Founders have had the time to assemble this enormous array of items in the few bells they had between the onset of the Healing and the boarding of the *Genesis*? As described in the Lex history? Or is that a fiction, too?

Lukas points to an entry in the upper right corner of the screen. It's tinier than the other entries, so I draw even closer to the Tech. "Do you see this?"

"Yes."

"What does it say?"

"It looks like a date."

"Exactly. What is that date?"

I look at the screen, then back at him. "That's two weeks before the Healing."

"Correct. Do you understand what that means?"

"Of course." If this wasn't so unbelievable, I'd be irritated at his question. Like I'm some sort of simple Maiden to whom he needs to explain everything. "It means that the Founders loaded the *Genesis* with all the necessary items for life two weeks *before* the Healing. Two weeks before the flood waters started rising."

"Exactly. All of your stories tell us that the flood waters were sudden and that the Gods selected the faithful to be saved. There wasn't a forewarning." There's contempt in his voice, especially the way he says the word *your*—as if he's exempting the Boundary.

"So The Lex is wrong," I say.

"Again."

"Again." Feeling a creeping sense of uncertainty, I pause for a tick. This Tech is telling us much more than the old tale about the inaccuracies of The Lex. "If it was just a simple matter of forewarning, the Founders could have written some passage about the Gods sending them a sacred message. To protect the faithful and all that. No, I think that this Manifest is telling us much more than that The Lex is wrong."

"What, then?" he asks.

The answer tumbles from my mouth before it is even fully formed, the words an avalanche of realization. "The Founders planned the settlement of New North long before the Healing. Think about how long it would have taken to assemble this list. Months, not weeks, I'm guessing. This is no mere forewarning. There are bigger questions at work here."

Lukas turns to me. "What questions?"

"Look at this." I point to a tiny entry at the bottom of the screen. "It says THE NEW NORTH COMPANY. Do you remember what you told me about a company?"

"Yes. That a company is a group of people who make something. Apple was the company that made Tech."

"Right."

He turns back to the screen. "So what exactly was the New North Company making with all these items? And

how did the Founders—or this New North Company—
know about the Healing long before it happened?"

I can't respond. I feel like the answers are so close, but
I can't reach them. Do they even really matter? I'm not
certain how the truth about the Healing and the founding
of New North will lead me to my brother's murderer, but
somehow I know this truth is intertwined with his death.
Perhaps that is also why I feel myself getting one step
closer to finding out what happened to Eamon.

"Do you think my brother knew about this?" I ask after
a tick.

"He never mentioned it to me. But maybe—"

I interrupt him. "Shh. I hear something." In the distance
a familiar sound. The clomp of the Archon Guards as they
tromp down a nearby corridor. They never bother to muf-
fle their heavy steps. Why should they?

I point at the ceiling. Lukas pulls out his *atlatl* and shoots
two lines into its icy expanse, one right next to the other.
He gestures for us to start climbing.

Hand over hand we ascend, my heart rattling in my
chest. I do my utmost to slow my breathing; I don't want
to give away our location by my panting. We pull our dan-
gling lines up as we climb until we can climb no more.
Lukas releases one of his hands to push my feet up against
the ceiling; I sink the toes of my bear-claw boots into its
surface. Lukas does the same just as the Guards scan the
floor of the Conservation Chamber with their forbidden
Tech-produced beams.

Together we cling to the ceiling like two spiders in the
center of an icy web.

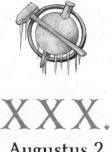

XXX.

Augustus 2
Year 242, A.H.

Even though I'm bleary-eyed from lack of sleep, I am ready and waiting when my parents take their seats at the breakfast table. They look surprised when my plate is cleared of the morning repast of broth and bread; usually they have to prompt me to eat. When I have my sealskin overcoat on before my father dons his, they laugh at my eagerness. But they misunderstand it. I'm racing to the Hall of Archons not because I long to resume my duties but because I have to make sure Lukas and I left no trace behind in our haste to escape.

In the Main Chamber, I arrange myself near the hallway leading to the Conservation Chamber. When my father calls the Archons to prayer, I dutifully chant "Hail to Sun the Mother," but my mind is retracing every step Lukas and I took last night. Archon Theo has eagle eyes.

The very tick my father ends the prayer, I'm gone. Thank the Gods I pass no one as I race down the corridor. I've got maybe five or six ticks until Archon Theo arrives. Turning the corner, I proceed under the entryway and cross into the Chamber and practically bump right into Theo.

How did he get in here before me? I just saw him in the Main Chamber. "Are you in a rush, Archon Eva?" he asks with a stern look.

"No, Archon Theo."

"I certainly hope that there's another explanation for your panting. You know my feelings about rushing."

"Of course, Archon Theo. Many times I've heard you say, 'Slow and steady wins the race.'"

"Indeed." He grins.

"Is that a phrase from The Lex? I don't remember seeing it, but maybe it's one of the lesser rules. I don't have those memorized."

"No, it's not." He scratches his head. "Funny, I'm not sure where it comes from."

"I've never heard your brother Archon Laurence use it."

"No." He gives me a sly grin. "But then he wouldn't use it, would he? Nothing slow or steady about him."

I glance around the room. There are scuffs in the usually polished ice floor, gouges in the ceiling, should anyone bother to look up, and one of the Tech is askew. Theo is always very particular about how we leave the Tech in the evening. I watch as he busies himself with getting on his sealskin gloves. His fear of the Tech hasn't diminished since our return to the Aerie; if anything, the constancy of contact has intensified it. Even within the safety of the

Conservation Chamber, and even though such a buffer can hinder our work, Theo takes every precaution to avoid touching the Tech directly.

Frantically pulling on the gloves Theo insists I wear, too, I walk with purpose but not haste over to the off-center Tech. Thank the Gods Lukas grabbed his charging contraption; no explanation would have sufficed for its presence. Just as I reach toward the Tech to straighten it, Theo asks, "What in the Gods are you doing, Archon Eva? We haven't gotten to those Relics yet in our cataloguing. We are still over here."

"My mistake, Archon Theo—"

"Wait a tick." He is staring at the ice-table behind me. "Why is that Tech misaligned?"

"I don't know."

His gaze shifts to mine. "You didn't dislodge the Tech from its normal position. I'm certain that you didn't."

"I don't think so, but it's possible I nudged it accidentally."

"No, that's not it," he says as he approaches. With his protective gloves in place, he runs his fingers across the ice-table. "Someone placed another object here." He points to the spot where Lukas had his charging machine. "It must have been last night. There is a slight indentation in the ice that can only be attributable to another object. Another *warm* object."

I remain motionless. I am frozen by my fear. Theo is piecing it all together. I will be found out for the fraud that I am—and get the gallows I deserve, according to The Lex. I will be made an example for all, like that poor Boundary worker. My mind utters a silent prayer. *By the Gods, whoever, whatever you are, please spare me. I seek only the truth.*

"I wonder . . ." he says, but not to me. He is staring off into the distance, his eyes glazed in a private rumination.

I don't want to ask, but know I must. "Wonder what, Archon Theo?"

"Nothing to trouble yourself about, Archon Eva." He gives me his brisk, officious smile. "You're probably right. You probably bumped into it. Let's spend the rest of today focusing on a far more important task—the sacred work of cataloguing the *Genesis* Relics. Only then can we begin the Chronicle."

XXXI.

Augustus 2
Year 242, A.H.

Even the numbing task of cataloguing every detail of the Tech doesn't calm my mind. I can't shake the idea that Archon Theo is trying to lure me into a confession with his uncharacteristic silence about the disrupted table. Normally he likes to discuss each theory that runs through his mind, and in truth, I learn much about reading Relics from this practice. That Theo would keep silent on a critical concern like the possible violation of the Tech is unthinkable. How could it be anything but a trap?

I leave in a dark fog. Fear consumes me as I enter my family home. I start up the stairs to change for dinner. I'm so distracted I almost miss Jasper waiting for me in the solar.

"Eva, my apologies for interrupting your thoughts," he says softly as he approaches the stairs.

"Oh, Jasper, I'm sorry that I didn't greet you properly. I'm . . . thinking of the Archon work I brought home with me." Smiling a little, I walk down the few steps that I've mounted and take his outstretched hand.

"Archon work is so important for the future of New North, Eva. Never apologize for doing your duty. I'll be disappointed if you leave the Archon world behind when you enter the doors of *our* home." He blushes a little when he says the phrase *our home*. I feel the heat rise in my cheeks as well. Soon our Union day will arrive and the departure to our own home with it, but truth be told, I've been so preoccupied since our Betrothal ceremony that I rarely think of it.

"Well, then, I promise to bring my Archon work home to *our* house," I say with a smile, reminded for the hundredth time how lucky I am to have a Betrothed so open in his views.

He lifts my hand to his lips. I think he's going to bestow the Gallant's kiss, but instead he turns over my hand. He traces my palm with his finger and then kisses the hollow. The sensation of his warm lips on my skin sends shivers through me. Has anyone seen this immodesty? For the first time since I arrived home, I realize we are completely alone.

I lead Jasper to the high-backed bench strewn with pillows embroidered by my mother. His face bears such an expression of longing that I almost abandon my intention to test his commitment—not to me, that's clear, but to the pursuit of the truth. But if not now, when?

I hold his hands tightly and ask, "Do you really want to hear of my work, Jasper?"

The hazy look slips away, and he takes a deep breath. "Yes. I want you to share everything with me."

"Do you recall our conversation yesterday about the distance to the Frozen Shores?"

His brow furrows. "Yes, the news was very disturbing."

"Right. But listen. That's not all. Not even close. That's just one of many disturbing things I've learned from the dig. One of many things that make me question what we've been told about New North. Do you remember the journal of Madeline?"

"The one you took from the Hall of Archons? Of course." It's a testament to his feelings for me that he's forgiven that outrageous breach of The Lex. And the lies I told him about it.

"Yes. Well, in it, Madeline tells a story about the objects she found on the *Genesis*, a tale that differs wildly from the official version she wrote in her Chronicle. One that details suspicions she had about the foundation of New North. Suspicions that she did everything in her power to repress when it came time to write her Chronicle."

Jasper laughs. "Her Chronicle? You mean that outlandish piece of fiction about finding Relics on the *Genesis* before it slipped away in a crevasse?"

I'm not laughing with him. My voice hardens. "I just came from the *Genesis*, Jasper. And everything that Madeline said—the reports that practically caused her to be shunned from Aerie life—were true."

"Your dig was on the *Genesis*?" He leans away from me. His face is incredulous.

"Yes. We uncovered all the artifacts that Madeline described and more. And I'm fairly certain that the story she wrote in her journal—the one containing questions about the creation of New North and The Lex itself—was more accurate than the Chronicle she submitted. The one that got her laughed out of Aerie society."

"By the Gods, Eva. Those are strong accusations. Are you sure?"

"I'm absolutely certain. I'm worried that the founding of New North—and The Lex along with it—is not as we've been told."

He removes his hands from mine. Glancing around the room, he says, "Be careful, Eva. You know better than anyone that such words are high treason."

"I don't utterly them lightly, Jasper. You know me well enough to believe that."

He reaches for my hands again. "I believe in you, Eva. I hope you have faith in that."

"It might be the only thing I have faith in these days."

"Eva, let me help you. And protect you if I can."

Jasper the Gallant has emerged. "I appreciate it, Jasper. But I don't need protection."

"I wouldn't be helping just for the sake of your protection, Eva. I want to uncover the truth, too. For all the Aerie. The Lex tells us that faith, loyalty, and truth are the cornerstones of our life in New North."

Ironic that Jasper is quoting The Lex in support of my efforts to upend *it*. "I don't want you to do anything to jeopardize your own safety."

"Eva, I will be helping you."

He says this, but he really has no sense of what he's getting into. I need to tell him at least some of the truth. "Madeline thought that the arrangement of artifacts on the deck of the *Genesis* looked like a setup. Like someone had very consciously scratched the Apple symbol on the Tech, started a first draft of The Lex, and then intentionally placed the two items next to each other to make it look like the conversion from the veneration of Apple to the worship of the Gods happened on the deck of the *Genesis*."

"So let me understand you. She thought the whole thing looked like a . . ." Jasper struggles to find the right word for this abomination. "Fiction?"

I know this is hard for him. "Yes, Jasper. I'm really sorry."

He inhales deeply and squares his shoulders. His face again assumes his typical Gallant expression, but his eyes bear none of the trusting innocence I normally see in them. "What can I do?"

"As a contestant in the Forge, you're given access to the Lexor vaults, right?"

"Yes, but it's limited. We're only allowed to look at past Forge competitions to prepare for the ritual."

"When you are in the Vaults, can you look for any documents related to the actual creation of the very first Lex? We might find some evidence related to Madeline's theories."

"If that's what you need, Eva." He sounds tired. In the long, silent tick that follows, I can almost see him trying to make this Lex-breaking part of his Gallant code. Finally he draws a breath. "The people of New North deserve the truth about the Healing, The Lex, everything. If we've been lied to by our Founders, we need to discover the deception and tell the Triad."

I nod. How I admire Jasper's scruples. I don't have the heart to tell him that I suspect the responsible party is the Triad itself.

XXXII.

Augustus 3–10
Year 242, A.H.

I slide back into routine. I spend days in the Hall of
Archons meticulously noting every detail of the Tech
at Archon Theo's instruction. I while away evenings at
home dining with my parents, Jasper, and Jasper's parents.
I feign interest in being a Maiden and an Archon and the
details of my Union, all the while thinking about something
else. How I can get back into the Conservation Chamber at
night. With Lukas.

It's been eight days since Lukas and I raced out of the
Hall of Archons in the dead of night. Eight days of waiting
for Theo to accuse me of breaking into the Hall. Eight days
of pining to get back in to examine the Tech alone, no matter the risk.

"Eva, are you listening?" my mother chides me from

across the crowded table. A large group has gathered for a feast before the Northern Lights festival. It's considered good luck to see the Northern Lights the first night they are out, and it's always a happy occasion, a night of revelry for all the people of New North.

"Yes, Mother. You and Lady Charlotte were discussing the Union Feast." I hadn't heard a word of their conversation, but I venture a guess. This is their latest topic, since the Union dress is now in its final stages. They talk of little else.

"Which of the desserts would you prefer?"

"Um, the honey cake." Even though the Testing ruined my taste for sweets, this was known to be my favorite treat.

"As I suspected, you weren't really listening to us. Honey cakes are not even one of the choices, Eva. They're too commonplace. We were thinking of pears in red wine or spiced dates stuffed with goat cheese." My mother's tone makes clear she isn't happy at this show of un-Maidenly behavior in front of Lady Charlotte.

The Gentlemen and Lords push back their chairs from the dining table and gesture for the Gentlewomen and Ladies to rise. Jasper sidles up to me as we wander into the solar for nuts and cheeses. "I haven't found any early records of The Lex yet," he whispers as he reaches for my hand.

"None?" I try not to sound disappointed. How did I think that in eight days Jasper would find damning evidence that The Lex was just some construct of the Founders instead of divine inspiration? A secret—if true—that's been hidden for nearly two hundred and fifty years? Ridiculous.

"But I did find a small group of documents stored under the heading *Genesis*," he adds. "Just a few pages, really."

"The *Genesis*?" The sudden surge of excitement makes

it hard to keep my voice steady and quiet. I link my fingers with his. Jasper has proven himself to be so brave and supportive in this dangerous venture, well beyond what I expected from him.

"Yes, but here's the strange thing about the documents. I read them, and they didn't really make any sense. They didn't have anything to do with the Founders' ship. Or Madeline's earlier discovery."

I search his eyes. "What were they about?"

"They seemed to be excerpts from a story, maybe some kind of fiction. It was an odd tale about a man and a woman named Adam and Eve who were in a garden . . . I think it was called Eden."

Jasper's description reminds me of something familiar, something at the edge of my memory. "Hmm. Adam and Eve and a garden. How do you know the pages were part of a larger story?"

"Because they were torn out of another book. Something called the Bible?"

I squeeze his hand tighter. That word! I can never forget it. Lukas found a copy of the Bible on Elizabet's computer, and he explained to me that it was the pre-Healing's version of The Lex. That the two books bear uncanny similarities to one another supports Madeline's suspicions that The Lex is man-made, not divine. "You're certain it was the Bible?"

"Yes, the first page said 'Bible' front and center. The heading on the page actually said *Genesis*, but there's no reference to the Founders' boat."

I am quiet.

Now he's searching *my* eyes. "Does the word *Bible* mean something to you?"

I'm not sure how far down into this I can pull Jasper just yet. "Possibly. But I have to do a little digging. I wish I could have seen those pages."

He smiles that beautiful, wide grin he saves for the most special of occasions. "May I kiss you later if I've made your wish come true?"

I smile back at his Gallant's flirtation and feign a curtsy. "Of course, kind sir."

He bows before me to kiss my extended hand and slips an envelope into my other one. "It seems as though I've granted your wish. And later I'd like you to grant mine."

My mother and Lady Charlotte motion for me to join them on the bench. Gallants and Lords traditionally sit separately from Maidens and Ladies after dinner. Jasper and I are violating that rule, a breach of decorum they can chalk up to Betrothal enthusiasm. Besides, it's the kind of breach my mother secretly approves of, even encourages. It shows that I truly am a Maiden. I take my place, tucking the envelope into the folds of my gown. While the Ladies chatter on about their own gowns for the Union, the Attendants serve the nuts and cheeses. A platter appears before me.

"Maiden Eva?" an Attendant asks.

I nod, and as the Attendant passes me a small plate, she whispers, "Tomorrow night, at the Hall."

I look up, confused by her words. It is Ana. It seems Lukas has finally sent me a message.

XXXIII.

Augustus 10
Year 242, A.H.

"Shall we ready ourselves for the festival?" my father asks as the conversation dies down, although it's not really a question. His suggestions are nearly always commands.

The group assembles in the solar as we bundle for the evening cold. Because the streets will be alive with other Northern Lights revelers, my mother selects her finest furs and instructs Katja to wrap me in mine.

We step out into a rare world of nighttime merriment. The normally pitch-black streets are bright with torches and packed with people. The Keeps have set up makeshift stands everywhere, offering samplings of savories and sweets. The favorite is always the Aurora Borealis, icicles drizzled with the purest honey. I decline, but Jasper takes one and licks it with the gusto of a child.

I giggle. He glances up with a goofy grin, and for a tick, he looks like Jasper the Schoolboy, tagging after my brother. His face distracts me from my thinking on Ana's message and his news about the *Genesis*.

We head toward the town square along with the rest of New North. The Northern Lights festival is one of the few attended by Aerie and Boundary alike, so the streets are doubly crowded. Amidst all the black-haired and dark-eyed Boundary folk, I keep thinking I see Lukas. But I don't. Maybe it's just as well. I wouldn't know how to act around him in public. Especially not with my arm linked with Jasper's.

At my mother's prompting, our parents take a prime spot in the town square; she doesn't like to miss a chance to be at the center of any gathering. We stand right next to the dais where the Chief Basilikon offers his annual Northern Lights festival blessing. "Let us look upon this display as another sign of mankind's second chance after the Healing, a symbol of the chosen people."

The crowd cheers and converges around us.

I lose sight of my parents in the throngs, and Jasper takes my hand in his own sticky glove. I assume he's just protecting me Gallantly, but to my astonishment, he leads us right past the dais and the Basilikon and out of the town square entirely.

Looking over his shoulder, Jasper shoots me a mischievous grin, one I didn't ever expect to see on his Gallant face. He leads us down an alleyway and up a set of stairs.

I'm disoriented at first. It's not until we ascend the steps that I realize we are on the roof of his family's Keep. And that no one in New North has a better view of the Northern Lights.

He draws close to me and reaches his arm across my shoulder. "Is this all right?"

I smile over at him. "It's better than all right."

We stare up at the heavens. The sky begins to glow phosphorescent. A faint green stripe fans across the horizon, then thickens. It starts to swirl, and hints of white and purple emerge, pulsating across the horizon. Suddenly a swath of pink, a shade not unlike Elizabet's backpack, but not nearly as brassy, appears, and the whole display of lights shimmers. The stars stretch endlessly above the colorful spectacle, the North Star glittering brightest among them.

No matter how many times I witness the Northern Lights, I am moved.

Tears stream down my face. Part of me is so happy to share this moment with Jasper, a small tick of simple joy amidst all the deception. Part of me is bereft at the sacrifice and fear and searching still ahead.

"Why are you crying?" Jasper asks, wiping away a nearly frozen tear from my cheek.

"Just some old memories."

"Of Eamon?"

I scramble for an innocent excuse. "Actually, of my Nurse Aga."

"I remember her."

"You do?" I'm surprised that a Boundary person would linger in an Aerie memory other than my own.

"Of course. She was always in the background when you and Eamon were little. Always smiling at you two."

"She was, wasn't she?" I think of her kindly, worn face. "On the night of the Northern Lights festival, she would tell Eamon and me a story, a different one than the Basil-kon tells."

"What was it?"

"She said that a long time before the Healing, a different great flood swept over the earth. The Gods spared a simple, pure race of people in the North from this deluge. When the flood waters finally receded, the Gods told these people to gather their things and follow Them to the North to new lands. The people listened, but became scared as they made the trek North because the sun was hidden behind the clouds. The Gods decided to cover the Northern cap of the world with great crystals of ice, some as high as mountains. With those crystals, the Gods were able to capture the rays of the hidden sun and reflect them up in the sky, giving their people a light to see by. And that is how the Northern Lights came into being."

Jasper stares up at the sky. "That's kind of beautiful," he says quietly.

"I know. I like it a whole lot better than the Basilikon's reason for the Northern Lights."

"Me, too." He glances down, shaking his head. "I don't know what to believe anymore. A few months ago, I would've thought that your nurse's story was some simple-minded Boundary notion. Now I'm not sure."

Am I really hearing that Jasper questions the very same things I do? I venture a Lex-breaking question. "Do you ever think that The Lex itself might be a fiction?"

He looks up, alarmed. Have I gone too far? "A fiction?"

"Not a fiction in the banned-story sense. Maybe that's the wrong word. More that . . . maybe it was crafted by the Founders to make us believe what they wanted us to believe."

"Are you saying that it wasn't Gods-inspired?"

I tread carefully. "I'm not saying that there aren't truths in it. In fact, I think there are. I believe that the Gods come to us in ways we're capable of understanding at a particular time. And that history as the Founders tell it might be . . . well, it might not have happened entirely the way they tell it."

He pauses for an eternal tick. "But you *do* think there are Gods-ly truths in The Lex mixed in with the Founders' other agendas?"

"I . . . do." I shrug, as if the notion hasn't been preoccupying me for weeks now. "It's just a thought. I might be wrong."

Jasper doesn't answer. He's staring up at the Northern Lights but seems to be looking through them. I wonder what he's thinking. It's hard to imagine that I ever thought he might have killed Eamon.

As if he can hear my thoughts, he turns to me and says, "Just about the only thing I believe in right now is you."

I am so torn by his response and his slightly shell-shocked look, that I feel like melting into the ice. What have I done to the loyal, Lex-abiding Gallant that Jasper used to be? I've crushed his faith, and what if I'm wrong? I'm just guessing at the truth.

Still, a part of me delights in his words. He is starting to question the same things I am, and to believe in the same things I do—and that makes me believe in him. I turn and look into his eyes. Instead of their normal clear blue, they glow green and purple and pink from the reflection of the Northern Lights. "Me, too."

Jasper pulls me close, bringing his lips to nearly touch mine. Then asks, "May I collect on the kiss you promised?"

"Of course."

I bring my lips to his. All thoughts of The Lex and the Founders and the *Genesis* and Madeline wash away from my mind, and I can think of nothing but him.

XXXIV.

Augustus 10
Year 242, A.H.

I finally retire to my bedroom, spent from the Northern Lights festival. Good thing Lukas didn't send word to meet tonight. Tomorrow night I might be ready. But tonight, I'm not certain I can tear myself away from the memory of my kiss with Jasper.

I shoo Katja away from my bedroom; I want to be alone with the feeling of Jasper's lips on mine. As I collapse onto my bed, an envelope slides out of my pocket. How could I have forgotten it even for a few ticks? Once again, I'm amazed at the dangerous lengths Jasper has gone to for me. Stealing these *Genesis* documents out of the Lexors' archives could have gotten him sent to the gallows.

I smile a little, thinking of his heroic acts—all for

me—as I delicately remove the few yellowing pages that I find inside the envelope and begin to read. The words are strange and oddly entrancing. They sound like certain sections of our Lex—the parts about our history, not the rules—and yet they are a doorway to a world that seems ancient and otherworldly. So different than any we learned about in School.

This *Genesis* starts with the creation of the world and the first humans, Adam and Eve, by a single God. They live in a perfect place called the Garden of Eden. The archaic-sounding story gets more interesting when a serpent appears in the garden.

In response to the serpent's question as to whether they could eat from every tree in the garden, Eve said, "We may eat of the fruit of the trees in the garden. But of the fruit of the tree of knowledge which is in the midst of the garden, God hath said, 'Ye shall not eat of it, neither shall ye touch it, lest ye die.'"

The serpent responded, "Ye shall surely not die: For God doth know that in the day ye eat thereof, then your eyes shall be opened, and ye shall be as gods, knowing good and evil."

When the woman saw that the tree was good for food . . . and a tree to be desired to make one wise, she took of the fruit thereof, an apple, and did eat, and gave also unto her husband with her, and he did eat. And the eyes of them both were opened, and they knew that they were naked . . .

They heard the voice of the Lord God . . . and he said,

"Hast thou eaten of the tree, whereof I commanded thee thou shouldest not eat?" . . .

The man said, "The woman whom thou gavest to be with me, she gave me of the tree, and I did eat . . ."

The woman said, "The serpent beguiled me, and I did eat . . ."

And the Lord God said, "Behold, the man is become as one of us, to know good and evil: and now, lest he put forth his hand, and take also of the tree of life, and eat, and live forever, he shall be banished."

Therefore the Lord God sent him forth from the garden of Eden, to till the ground from whence he was taken.

I sit up on my bed. What is this strange world of Eden? Did it exist in the pre-Healing world? And what became of this Adam and Eve? Is this fiction or some account that's meant to be true? From the text, I cannot tell. We don't have stories of the first humans in The Lex, just the tale of the pre-Healing world and our second chance in New North. But what seems to be clear—fiction or truth—is that someone, sometime recounted a story about a single God who gave these first humans a paradise in which to live, from which they were exiled when they defied this God's only rule: to keep away from the fruit born from the tree of knowledge.

Apples. Can it really be a coincidence?

As I read the pages over and over, trying desperately to make sense of them, the story becomes more and more

familiar. Pieces of it, anyway. Suddenly I remember where
I had heard it before. My childhood Nurse Aga used to tell
me a version of it, along with all sorts of wild tales that were
banned in the Aerie. The image and idea that the mere fact
of a woman biting into a piece of fruit would open her eyes
to forbidden knowledge and change the fate of the world
made such an impact on me that years later, I included an
image of a bitten apple in a piece of embroidery I worked
on for the Basilika. This deviation from the accepted sym-
bolic forms was considered so heretical that I was removed
from the Maidens' sewing circles and sent to work in the
Ark. Ironically it was a punishment that served me well, as
I adored the Ark, much to my mother's chagrin.

Another question nags at me: Why is this story in a Bible
section called *Genesis*? Did this have any relationship to the
Founders' ship *Genesis*? It must.

I feel like answers lie in these pages, but I cannot see the
connections.

I turn my attention to the scrawled notes in the pages'
margins, holding them close to the candlelight. The handwriting is so different than the form we use in the Aerie
that I can't make sense of it first. Plus it varies slightly from
comment to comment. Clearly, different people annotated
the *Genesis* story, and I must deal with each note separately.
Only when I transcribe the handwriting letter by letter can
I decode it.

Should we include an Eden tale in The Lex? Might be
too memorable for the Christian people to forget. And
not enough similar stories throughout cultures to make
it a monomyth that other religious groups represented in
New North would embrace. Thoughts?

✧

Maybe we should take a symbol from the Eden story for The Lex? If Eve's bitten fruit is an apple, and we liken past people's addictive use of technology to worship of "false god Applo." It works well with the Apple technology, after all. Then by use of the bitten apple symbol, we subtly suggest that by 'biting of the Apple Tech' the people are partaking of evil? And that this led to mankind's Fall and the Healing? Just like in Eden.

✧

This might work well to suggest mankind is responsible for the Healing, and that humans must make sure they don't bite the Apple again—namely, partake of anything modern—or risk another Healing. This would lead the people to the logical conclusion that, if we follow God's mandates this time, God might let us stay in this para-dise/utopia of New North. Unlike the pre-Healing people, and before them, Adam and Eve. Does this work? Too heavy-handed?

✧

Not at all. We will create our own Eden in New North where we all have what we need as long we don't 'bite the Apple' again.

With this last note, I understand. Not that the revelation brings me any joy or peace. The theory I'd only speculated

about with Jasper was correct. New North and The Lex—
and everything about our entire history and world—is a
lie. Worse, it is fiction of the most evil sort: the kind that's
dressed up as the truth.

XXXV.

Augustus 11
Year 242, A.H.

"I think you can start your Chronicle this afternoon, Archon Eva," Theo says as I'm entering a note in the log on the eighth piece of Tech from the *Genesis* dig. At first I think I misheard. I'm deep into a query about whether this Relic's slightly more silvery sheen is attributable to weathering or the original patina application. In fact, I couldn't possibly have heard him correctly.

"I'm sorry, Archon Theo. Do you mind repeating what you just said?"

"I said, I think you can start your Chronicle of the *Genesis* this afternoon."

"I don't understand. It is yours to write." It's unheard of for the junior Archon to take the lead on the Chronicle. Like everything else in New North society, status prevails.

He offers an encouraging smile. "We only have seven days until the Founders' Day celebration. You heard the announcement at this morning's gathering; the Chief Archon would like a commemoration of the *Genesis* excavation and its Relics at that celebration. The whole population will be in attendance, after all. I think you need to start working on it if it's to be completed in time."

"You want *me* to write it?" I have to ask the question out loud. I am incredulous.

Folding his arms over his generous belly, he says, "I may be a proud Archon, but I'm not so arrogant that I can't admit when one of my fellow Archons has a gift that I do not. Archon Eva, the Gods gave you the gift of writing. I may be able to cobble together an exacting description of a Relic and its pre-Healing purposes, but I've never been able to captivate the people like you did with your Testing Chronicle. And the Founders' Day celebration is a time for captivation."

I bow my head in acceptance of his praise, a Maidenly gesture I can't seem to shake. "Thank you for your kind compliments, Archon Theo. But I'm wondering whether Archon Laurence approves of this selection. I don't want to challenge your authority, but he is in charge of the *Genesis* excavation, and his dislike of me is ill-concealed."

Theo smiles again. It's warmer, more open, somehow disconcerting. "I don't tell my brother everything, Archon Eva. We all have our secrets regardless of The Lex, don't we?"

I freeze. Secrets again. He's pretty much repeated verbatim what I can only construe as a veiled threat. Or am I misreading him? Just when I'd stopped waiting for him to accuse me of breaking into the Conservation Chamber that night, he speaks again of secrets.

He stands there, anticipating some sort of response from me. I'm debating whether he's awaiting my acceptance of his assignment or my reaction to his cryptic reference when he says, "Your answer?"

"I'd be honored. Just as long as Archon Laurence won't be"—I struggle to find a word to describe the breadth of his unpleasantness and settle on—"unhappy when he finds out?"

"Why don't you leave the details of that up to me, Archon Eva. You keep your focus on the Gods-given task of writing the Chronicle, all right?"

"Yes, Archon Theo. Thank you for the privilege." I bow once more. "Would you like to discuss it before I begin?"

"I leave the writing to you." He pauses for a tick, then says, "But I will share with you what I felt when I first saw the main deck of the *Genesis* and all that Tech, in case it bears on your decision about how to frame your work. I felt gratitude. Gratitude that our Founders were brave enough to reject the only deity they'd ever known—Apple—and to embrace the true Gods. If they hadn't been so courageous, mankind would not have been granted a second chance. We wouldn't be standing here today."

Admiring Theo as I do, even liking him, it's hard for me to listen to him without wanting to scream the truth at the tops of my lungs. But I must remain silent if I am to do my duty. So I lock up the real story of New North and its Gods deep inside, knowing that I can only reveal the truth to Theo at the same time I share it with the rest of our island.

This liberty I'm being granted is unusual; only in the Testing do young people write Chronicles. Possibilities drift through my mind as we walk through the labyrinthine corridors to the Scriptorium. Only when we arrive, when I see the tools I need to write, does one particular idea take hold. One that may make Theo lament his decision when he hears it read aloud. The truth can be bitter. But empty lies are far worse.

I will draft a Chronicle that honors Madeline's discovery in the hull of the *Genesis* and vindicates her quashed suspicions. One that honors Elizabet and all the voices silenced by history, and one that resurrects them. One that will cause a furor in those who know the truth—and serve as a trap for the one who killed my brother.

XXXVI.

Augustus 11
Year 242, A.H.

Once again, I find myself sneaking out of my home,
in violation of The Lex. But am I really? I am an
Archon. I have the right to move about in ways
that other Maidens, or even Gallants and Ladies, do not.
Even though bells have passed since the Vespers Bell
sounded, and the doors of the Aerie have all closed for
the night, I feel an urge to walk right out the front door
and stroll down the streets, as is my Gods-given right as a
member of the Triad.

But I'd be lying if I did so. I'm not venturing out of my
home in my capacity as an Archon, and so I cannot tempt
the Gods, or whoever oversees our world. I cannot lie in
that regard if I am to serve the truth. No, I must lie in other
ways.

I must arrive at the Hall of Archons when the moon stands at its peak, so I slip out of my house by way of the icy turret walls once again. Funny how a route that once felt dangerous now seems commonplace.

Devoid of people, the streets glisten in the moonlight like the sleeping castle in a forbidden tale told to me once by my Nurse Aga. For the second time since my return from the Testing, I am alone wandering down the ghostly white streets, enjoying my solitude. I pass the tower I stood upon with Jasper and pause to look at it from the outside, thinking again about the Northern Lights festival—

Foolish.

The light from the Guards' torches creeps around the corner just before it hits the toe of my *kamiks*. How could I be so stupid to forget for one tick to keep watch for the rounds of the Ring-Guards? Crouched down low, I wait for any sight or sound of the Guards to pass.

Once I'm certain that they've moved on, I race down the street and across the square to the Hall of Archons. At least I'm no longer daydreaming. Near the back wall, Lukas is waiting, a dark shadow against the endless whiteness of the Aerie.

"Where have you been?" he demands. His black eyes betray a mixture of concern and irritation. Even though Lukas can sit for an entire *sinik* over a seal hole waiting for the perfect moment to harpoon a surfacing seal, he never shows patience with me. Not that I can blame him in this instance.

"I had to wait out the Ring-Guards' rounds." I don't want to tell him that I almost got spotted. Confessing would give voice to the reason why: I lost focus because I was thinking about Jasper. He nods, though his face is cloudy and uncertain. Without speaking, we get out our equipment. I hand Lukas a sealskin rope, and he shoots the line over the wall. We strap on our bear-claw boots and hook onto it. Raking over the slick wall to give it a rougher texture, we begin to climb. We act in unison as though we are one instead of two, the way we were right after Eamon's death. For a brief instant, I am almost comforted.

The moment we crest the wall, I take the lead. Since Lukas's fall through the intentionally thin section of the roof—a booby trap, no doubt—I've been studying the ceiling, marking possible pitfalls. The study has paid off. Mere ticks later we are lowering our lines down the interior wall and dropping into the Yard. After we hide all evidence of our presence, I take Lukas by the hand, wordlessly leading him through the warren of corridors to the Conservation Chamber. I light my *naneq*, and a silvery glow fills the room. There all the Tech awaits.

Lukas jumps to rush to it, but I place a hand on his shoulder. With my other hand, I motion for him to pause. Reaching into my pack, I slide out a piece of fabric and place it next to the Tech. I want no sign of Lukas's charger left for Theo to find in the morning.

The rooms brightens further as Lukas powers up the first Relic. Over his shoulder, I see a dizzying array of small squares appear on the screen. It's clear that he knows precisely which one to examine; he returns to the Manifest we'd been examining last time.

As he scrolls down the pages of the document, I ask him questions about the entries. My inquiries must be annoying him, because he whispers, "Why don't you do some investigation in one of the other rooms? I'll come to get you if I find anything new."

"Lukas, this is what we came to find. I want to be here for any discoveries."

"Eva, you are losing out on the chance to uncover something else that might be important. Remember how I told you that some of the answers we seek might be in archives? In the oldest documents, not the Tech? Why don't you look there?"

I don't like being dismissed, but he makes a point. The Vault is nearby, and I've always wanted access without the unblinking stare of the Scribe. "All right. But the tick you find—"

"I'll come for you. I promise. Just tell me how to get there."

I acquiesce in as few words as possible, then pad down the hallway and up the stairs. Passing by the open doorway to my father's office, however, I hesitate. I've never been inside. Our paths rarely cross in the Hall of Archons after the morning prayer. I certainly have no official reason to be in the Chief Archon's office.

I peek through the doorway. A large wooden desk and chair preside over the room with cold authority. A diptych bearing emblems of the Gods sits in the corner, a prayer mat humbly set before it. Scrolls are strewn on the desk and work table, and on the wall hangs a document. It's not part of The Lex; it's something I've never seen.

Curious, I draw closer and hold my *naneq* to it.

It is my father's Chronicle—the very one that won him the Chief Archon seat. Usually, Chronicles are stored in the vault after each Testing year, but he must have received permission to hang his on the wall once his term began. My eyes narrow and my heart begins to pound. I've heard stories about his excavation of the mirror Relic, but I've never seen the actual Chronicle or heard it read aloud before.

THE CHRONICLE OF TESTOR JON
Year 218, A.H.

On first glance, the artifact seems ordinary, unworthy of the Relic title. Consisting of a large oval attached to a narrow rectangle, the simple black object is unadorned, made only of that artificial pre-Healing material called Plastic. As its function and purpose are unknown but seemingly plebeian, most Testors would pass it over in favor of some more worthy artifact.

Why did I linger? What called me to lift this artifact from its icy grave and turn it over? The Gods.

The Gods Themselves whispered that I should pause. They murmured for me to remove my chisel from my belt and unearth this item They breathed that I should take care. Of course, I listened.

I knelt over the object. Bit by bit, I loosened the artifact from the ice's hold. When I sensed that I could remove the item without harming it, I raised it from the floor of the cave. As I stared at the black Plastic artifact, I wondered why the Gods called me to excavate it, so uninteresting it appeared.

And then I turned it over.

A face stared back at me. Frightened beyond words at this spawn of Apple, I confess that I screamed and dropped the item on the cave floor. I retreated to the far reaches of the cave, terrified beyond reason. What should I do?

"Be brave, for We are with you." I heard the words of The Lex aloud as if the Gods were in the cave alongside me, answering my question.

I dared to move close to the object again. Hand shaking, I lifted the artifact from the floor. The face gazed back at me. Steeling myself against Apple's wiles, I examined it. The face was not static, like the paintings and other depictions we see on the walls of the Basilika or in the weavings of our Maidens and Gentlewomen and Ladies. It moved of its own accord, eyes blinked, eyebrows lifted, mouth opened and closed, nostrils flared. What evil trick was this? I wondered.

I breathed deeply, reminding myself of the Archons' teachings and the Gods' presence. Extending a finger, I reached out to touch the artifact. To my amazement, it touched me back. Each motion I made, by face or hand, the being within the artifact imitated.

At that tick, I realized that the face and the hands were not a creation of Apple. They were my own.

And I understood then that this was no ordinary artifact, but a Relic indeed. The only one of its kind that exists in the world after the Healing. This was a Relic of legend: a Mirror.

This Relic is so emblematic of the depravity and self-centeredness of the pre-Healing people that it merits a mention in The Lex itself. All New Northerners are familiar with The Lex's explicit ban on Mirrors: "Make no Mirrors and let none pass before your eyes, as they are the embodiment of Vanity." All New Northerners have heard the Basilikons sermonize on the way in which Vanity led to the downfall of the pre-Healing people, their women in particular. So obsessed did the females become with their appearance, they began to worship their so-called beauty above all else: they even created businesses and industries dedicated to fashioning and preserving it. Women's attractiveness became a false deity unto itself, a minion of Apple.

Even in our own time, the world after the Healing, we have seen evidence of the evil power of Vanity. The first and only female Testor, Madeline, became so enamored of her own image that she fabricated her Chronicle. In her desperate attempts to win the Archon Laurels and heap honors upon herself, she claimed that she found her Apple altar on the deck of the Genesis.

If her claims were true, where was the famed ship that brought the first Founders to New North? When Archons returned to the Testing Site to investigate her allegations, the Genesis was nowhere to be found. Only a gaping hole. This vanity, inherent in all women, is only one reason that females should never be permitted to become Testors. They are too easily swayed by the whispers of Apple to be trusted with this sacred duty; they are too weak of mind, body, and spirit to Test.

It is this exact Vanity that the Gods caution us against in The Lex. It is this same sin that They warn us against now with this unearthing of the Mirror Relic. Let us heed the warnings of the Gods and remember the importance of our commitment to this Lex-life of New North. This is our second, and only, chance.

Praise be to the Gods and the Testing.

I shrink back from the wall. At first I rub my eyes, half-expecting to wake up in my bed at home. Everything has a dreamlike quality in the dim light of the *naneq*: this parchment, this chamber, this moment. I can't believe that these are the words of my father. How could the same man who wrote those words about Madeline—about all women, really—be the same encouraging, loving, and supportive father that I know? No wonder it was so hard for him to watch me walk through the Hall of Archons on that very first day; he doesn't believe women should be here in the first place. He has much in common with my mother. But at least she makes her motives known, even when she's trying to conceal them.

Do I really know my father at all? Where does the truth lie?

I want to fold myself into a corner of my father's office and cry. No one is what or who they seem. Not my father, not the Triad, not the Founders, not even New North itself. In what—or whom—can I believe?

It doesn't matter. I remind myself of my mission to find out who killed my brother. Eamon's death has brought me here. I can't look back now. I owe it to him to deliver the truth. I summon my courage and anger and hurry from the office down the hallway to the Vault.

The *naneq* seems brighter in this dark place. Maybe it's just my imagination. But the shelves feel as if they open themselves, spreading out before me, offering their wares like Keepers on Market Day. I try to focus on making a fruitful selection.

The oldest documents are stored in the far back corner.

I pass the empty perch of the Scribe and traverse the long length of the Vault. Since no window cutouts dot the walls, no moonlight can reach here. The corner is very dark, nearly the pitch-black of Lukas's eyes, and I have to turn up my *naneq* to an uncomfortably bright level to see anything.

At first, all I can make out are shelves of colorful book spines. Bright blue, deep red, even a vivid green. The very presence of these books is an oddity in New North. Most Archon documents take the form of tiny bird-delivered scrolls or newly bound papers reused from pre-Healing books. Scarcity of paper necessitates this destruction. Books like these certainly date from before the Healing and in the normal course of things would have been utilized many times over.

What is so special about these? So critical that someone powerful would have ordered their preservation for centuries?

Lettering decorates several of the spines, and I bring my *naneq* near. Strange names adorn them: *Pali Canon, The Book of the Dead, Njáls Saga, A Compendium of Greek and Roman Mythology, The Gnostic Gospels, Folktales of Celtic Ireland* among them. I will ask Lukas if he is familiar with any of them; the names hold no meaning for me.

Because so many bear the title *Pali Canon*, I slide out one of these first, and decades of dust slide out along with it. Blowing the dust away and delicately opening the ancient text, I find a script I've never encountered. Poor first choice. Reaching for another volume, this one entitled *The Odyssey*, I am pleased to find English words in the pages. I open to a part of the story in which a raft someone named Odysseus has built to sail home is destroyed by a sea god named Poseidon. Interesting, but the tale is long, and I need to assess the other texts. I return it to the shelves.

I turn my attention to an entire shelf of animal hide–bound books that bear no name at all. Pulling out the first one, I find familiar language on the first page; it is nearly verbatim the opening lines from the Biblical story *Genesis*. A thought occurs to me, and one after the other, I take these unnamed books from the shelf.

They are all versions of the Bible.

Now I understand this protected corner of the Vault. It houses a collection of epic fictions—and perhaps epic truths—of stories and legends from people who lived before the Healing . . . from *all* people. Were these tales used like the *Genesis* story had been? Considered for inclusion in some form in The Lex, and then ultimately rejected?

So many of them, their details lost to time. Buried like Relics by the Archons. And then excavated and retold in new forms, over and over again. My mind spins. But just as I'm about to page through yet another version of the Bible, I hear footsteps reverberate down the hall.

XXXVII.

Augustus 11
Year 242, A.H.

I pad down the stairs as quickly and quietly as my *kamiks* will allow. I've got to get to Lukas before the guards do. It's one thing if I'm found here after the None Bell, and quite another if Lukas is discovered. I think of when Jasper and I were caught and almost laugh. The claim that Lukas is my Betrothed won't work. A Boundary and Betrothed Maiden, conspiring together, trespassing on sacred ground? We'd both get the gallows. Terror melts the brief smile off my face.

The footsteps get louder. I crouch behind a doorway to the Restoration Chamber, praying that the Guards don't peek inside. The footsteps pause just outside, but then continue on toward the kitchens. Was I really quiet enough? Or were they so tempted by a late evening meal that they would forgo a thorough examination of their rounds? It seems too easy.

I finally exhale. Counting the ticks, I wait a quarter bell. Then I creep down the remainder of the hallway—and freeze.

It *was* too easy.

The Guards wait at the ready just outside the Restoration Chamber. Hands on their swords, they are ready to attack whomever they heard lurking in the room.

Their stances slacken when they see it's me. Confusion takes hold of their expressions, and they loosen their grip on their swords. I almost start to panic and run, but I know the only way out of this situation, if there is a way out, is directly through it. I scramble for an excuse for my presence in the Hall of Archons long past the nightly locking of its doors.

"Archon Eva. What are you doing here at this bell?"

I summon my most authoritative voice and posture and say, "Still working away on my Chronicle for the Founders' Day celebration. Holed up in the Scriptorium until it's done."

"You know the rules, Archon Eva," the taller one says. "All Archons must leave the Hall at the final bell."

"I know the rules, but I also know how important this Chronicle is to Archon Laurence and to Founders' Day. I missed the final bell because I was so engrossed in writing. I decided to stay through the night to finish my work. I'm sure you understand. And you know as well as I that I am not in violation of The Lex. There is no closing time specified therein. It is tradition, not law."

They glance at each other, clearly unsure as to how to proceed in this highly unusual situation. Besides, I speak the truth in terms of what is expressly forbidden, and my knowledge of The Lex is now legendary in the Aerie. I'm certain that these two don't know The Lex as well as I do. Conversely their knowing this about me frightens them, so they dare not question my pronouncement. They seem to reach an unspoken agreement, and the Guard who's been doing all the talking says, "We can let it go just this once, Archon Eva. But we must escort you to the front door of the Hall. We have rules to follow."

"Of course. Just as soon as I make safe my work in the Scriptorium. I will meet you at the doors in five ticks."

I can see they don't like leaving me alone in the Hall for even one more tick. But they are bound to *pareo*, too, and begrudgingly agree.

I walk quickly toward the Scriptorium, and once I'm out of the Guards' sight, I duck down the corridor to the Conservation Chamber. My heart is pounding, more out of fear than exertion. "The Guards found me," I whisper to Lukas.

He jumps up and starts grabbing his gear. "What are you doing in here, then?"

"I have to meet them in four ticks at the Hall doors. You have to leave now. I'll keep them distracted in the front while you climb over the back wall. If I can, I'll meet you back at the Clothing Keep."

Lukas waves me closer. "Take a quick look at this before I shut it off. You know how the Manifest shows that the Founders were stockpiling resources for at least two weeks before the Healing?"

"Yeah," I whisper back, my heart still thumping. I glance back toward the hall.

"Well, in the Boundary, we've heard rumors that the pre-Healing people had Tech that predicted the weather. I've been thinking maybe that's how they managed to come up with the lead time to stockpile the *Genesis*."

For the briefest tick, I'm so astonished that I forget my fear. Tech that predicts the weather? I can't imagine such a thing. But then I'm reminded of what Elizabet said in her video. "It makes sense, you know . . . remember how Elizabet questioned how her parents knew to evacuate so early? Long before the seas started to take over the shores. If predicting the weather was commonplace, then she wouldn't have wondered about that."

"That's true." He pauses as if to trying to determine where to place that piece of information in this huge, complicated puzzle. Whether he doesn't understand the need for haste or he's just confident in his own speed, he makes me want to scream.

Lukas turns back to the computer. The screen glows blue as his fingers dance on the rectangular squares. I kneel next to him, hoping he'll get the hint to stop this and run. Besides, all I see is a jumble of numbers and a diagram. He makes little noises, but whether they indicate understanding or confusion, I'm not sure. Either way, we need to leave. "Come on," I implore him.

"Just one last tick." He stops on one page and points. "See this drawing?"

"What am I supposed to see? We don't have much time."

"Doesn't it resemble some sort of weather gauge? And look. Along the margin, there's all sorts of notes about the depth of the ice and the strength of the currents."

I really can't see a gauge, but I examine the notations along the margins. They remind me of some earlier notes, ones that I disregarded on first glance. The pieces are coming together.

All at once, I stop breathing. *By the Gods . . .* It's my turn to delay. "Go back to the first screen, Lukas."

He returns to the first page. Was this the page I remembered? I scan down the page as quickly as I can. Yes, there are the notes.

In tiny lettering near the very bottom of the page, it says, *For more details on the early research behind this strategy, please reference "President Eisenhower's Science Advisory Committee on Weather Modification for Military Purposes, January 1958, Highly Classified," and "NATO's Von Karman Committee Report on Climate Change and Environmental Warfare, 1960, Highly Classified."*

My heart is beating very fast. "Look at the title, Lukas."

He leans closer to the screen, then glances up at me. His face is blank.

I don't want to say the words aloud, but it seems that I must. "The Founders didn't use this Tech to predict the weather. They used this Tech to cause the Healing."

XXXVIII.

Augustus 11
Year 242, A.H.

As I walk through the doors of the Hall of Archons and into the night, I wonder if the Guards will try to follow me. I can't be certain that they won't—for my own safety, I'm sure they would say if I spotted them—so I head toward home. Only when the streets are utterly silent, save the usual shifting of the ice, do I turn toward the Clothing Keep. And Lukas.

I am anxious; the ice clouds of my breath come thicker and faster than usual, ghostly tendrils in the moonlight. I can't stop thinking about what we'd read. We didn't even need to skim that much for the cryptic drawing and notations on the *Genesis* Tech to make sense. The Founders not only had the ability to predict the weather, they could also harness and control it. In the days and bells before the

Healing, the Founders, operating under their Pre-Healing name of the New North Corporation, used nuclear Tech to divert sea currents and melt the polar ice caps. The *Genesis* was fully loaded for a new life in New North not because the Founders knew that the Healing was imminent but because they caused it. They had been planning the Healing for years, if not decades.

As I navigate the dark streets of the Aerie, my thoughts are only half focused on the Ring-Guards' patrol and steering around the walkways' icy patches. My mind is brimming with certain terrible phrases from the reports: "presently within man's reach is the ability to manipulate climate for long periods" and "strategic multi-megaton nuclear detonation to alter the course of ocean streams and global weather patterns." The truth is more horrible than I could have ever imagined.

But I can't speak it aloud or even really think about it just yet. Even though Lukas and I didn't plan to rendez-vous, I need to see him.

Not until I reach the relative safety of Lukas's little room in the Clothing Keep do I allow myself to contemplate in full the horror of the truth. There in the relative warmth of his tiny chamber, in the flickering glow of its small fire—in the comfort of his arms—I can no longer stave off the inevitable.

I fall against him and gasp. "I can't believe it."

Lukas hugs me close and chokes out a "Neither can I." Even in his wildest speculations about the true history of New North, he could have never imagined this atrocity. Who could have?

A memory flashes through my mind. I recall the tick from the Testing when I stood on the Frozen Shores for the first time and fully comprehended the billions of people who died beneath the seas spread out before me. I think about Elizabet drowning in a flood engineered by her own parents, who were certainly Founders and part of the New North Corporation. The magnitude of that loss and horror of this truth melt my numbness, and I start to sob. "They killed billions of people. Not the Gods, the Founders. They killed their own children."

"Yes." Lukas's voice is as cold as the night air. "They acted like the Gods themselves."

I slide out of his arms, suddenly dizzy. I rush outside just before I start heaving. If I wasn't so distraught, I'd be embarrassed.

Once I'm finished, Lukas leads me back inside. Gently, he takes off my sealskin cloak, seats me in his single chair, and wipes down my face with a cloth he dips in water warming over the fire. "Are you okay?" he asks, kneeling beside me.

"I don't think I'll ever be okay again, Lukas." I take his hands in mine and ask a question I know he can't answer. "Why? Why did they do it?"

"I don't know. I can't imagine any rationale that would have made it seem reasonable. I can only guess that the Founders wanted to start over. Create a society that they thought was better than the pre-flood world—"

"At the expense of their children's lives?" I interrupt, angry at his words. My voice is loud, too loud for this tiny space in the darkest hour of the night.

He flinches. "Eva, I'm not saying that I agree with their reasons. I'm just guessing that's how they justified the floods to themselves. Sometimes people do awful things in the name of a greater good."

I hold his hands tighter. "I'm sorry."

He grips back. "I know. We are being asked to imagine the unimaginable."

"I don't think it was unimaginable to the Founders. In fact, they had been imagining it, planning it down to the tiniest detail, for years. It's the only explanation that makes sense. It's why they took such care in crafting The Lex. The Founders destroyed the old world so they could create the world *they* wanted. But they needed to make sure that the people would follow them. So they made the old world seem evil. They invented a fictional history so they could control New North. It's why they borrowed from the Bible and these other pre-Healing myths. They truly *did* try to become Gods, just the way they claimed Apple did. They created a past, present, and future to which the survivors of the Healing would cling. It's sickening."

Lukas nods. "I know." His voice is distant.

I stand up, leaving Lukas to kneel by my empty chair. I begin pacing the room. "Do you think that Eamon knew about this?"

"I don't know. He never said anything. But I'm guessing he got close to this truth."

"So somebody else out there knows the truth. And that person—or persons—are the ones that killed Eamon."

"Maybe." Lukas sounds distracted. "Eva, this is exactly the kind of answer the *Angakkuq* would seek. The kind of information that would set all the people of New North free to create a real society where we lived by our own rules instead of the falsehoods of The Lex."

I stop pacing and glare at him. "Lukas, don't make this into something it's not. This is about finding Eamon's killer. Not fulfilling your fantasies about the *Angakkuq*."

"I know, Eva." He bites his lip, then meets my gaze. "But can't you see that they are one and the same? When you find out who knows the truth by telling the people of New North, you will also find Eamon's killer."

I know he is right on some level. But on another he is very wrong. This kind of belief at the expense of everything else was what led to the Healing in the first place. I don't want my search for my brother's killer to become intertwined with this role of *Angakkuq* he's foisted on me and knows I've rejected. I want retribution. Rather, I want justice. Eamon was another victim of the Founders as well. And then I want this painful sojourn into the past to be over. To return to normal, whatever that looks like now. Though I can't imagine returning to a world where the murdering Founders are toasted and praised and worshipped and quoted over and over again. Still, I'll deal with the uncertainty of the future when the time comes.

So I say, "I don't see how telling the truth to the people of New North would expose those who know it already."

"The ones who know the truth will try to stop you on Founders' Day." His tone is suddenly very certain, and very cold.

I wonder where he's hiding his concern for my well-being, or if he's even hiding it at all. "Why wouldn't they just let me speak and then sentence me to swing from the gallows?"

Lukas shakes his head. "Killing you would only make a martyr of you. It wouldn't erase what you say from people's minds. In fact, it would probably reinforce the possibility that you are speaking the truth."

"This will never work," I mutter, mostly to myself.

"Yes, it will. On Founders' Day, you are scheduled to

march to the center of the town square dais and read your Chronicle of the *Genesis* dig, right?"

"How do you know that?"

He smiles a little. "Did you forget that we Boundary have ears everywhere? Anyway, it makes sense that the Archons would want you to read. You are the crowd favorite."

I don't return his smile. "I can't promise that I'll be allowed to read. I am writing it, but I doubt Archon Laurence will let me present it to the people. The *Genesis* is his big find. It's his ticket to the Chief position when my father steps down."

"That may be, but I know you, Eva. You are resourceful. You will find a way to make this happen. It is too perfect. On Founders' Day, all of New North will be assembled in the Aerie Square. Instead of reading your Chronicle, you will read a statement of the truth. And before you get to the end—but not before the people begin to understand—someone will try to stop you."

Lukas's eyes look so steely and determined that he's starting to scare me a little. "Aren't you worried about me at all in this scheme of yours?" I ask. My voice sounds small in my ears.

Without warning, he rushes toward me. He grabs my hands and squeezes them tight. "I would never leave you exposed, Eva. My men will be on the Ring, watching everything. Protecting you."

"Your men?" I pull my hands free. Now he has "men"and "ears everywhere." Eamon's Companion. My family's servant. Since when? Suddenly I feel like a cog in a pre-Healing machine. Unaware of the greater workings and only important in a general sort of way. A replaceable sort of way.

"I am not the only seeker of the truth," Lukas continues, seeing the doubt and suspicion in my eyes. "There are so many Boundary like me who want to see the Aerie structure topple and New North change into a new, free society. How do you think we Boundary felt when your Founders landed on our island—the land we've lived on for thousands of years—and tried to tell us how to lead our lives?"

I'd never thought about it quite that way before. Shame at the presumptuousness of my people courses through me. Shame at my own haughtiness. "I can't imagine it," I whisper.

"When my grandmother called you the *Angakkuq* and told you that we've been waiting for you for generations, she was serious, Eva. My people have been waiting for the *apiqsaq*—helping spirit—of the *Angakkuq* since the Founders' ships landed on this shore. And we knew that this time was coming long before then, too."

I still can't bring myself to look at him directly. "You've never laid out the whole plan like this."

"I don't think I was ever really sure that we could uncover the truth. But you did it; you unearthed the buried secret." He wraps his arms around me so tightly I can hardly breathe. "You are more than I could have ever hoped or prayed for. And for that, I thank *my* Gods."

His words sound odd. But I let him pull me close again. I bury my head in his shoulder and squeeze my eyes closed. From within the depths of his arms, I ask, "Are you speaking to me as the *Angakkuq* or as Eva?"

He takes my head in his cold rough hands so that I have no choice but to stare into his black eyes. I feel a warmth spreading through me and am so conflicted. I want to be near him, but Jasper's face on the night of the Northern Lights festival keeps appearing in my mind.

Before placing his lips on mine, he says, "As everything."

XXXIX.

Augustus 13
Year 242, A.H.

I am alone with quills, ink, even fresh, unused paper. Silence pervades the empty chamber; Archon Theo wants to ensure that my creative gifts remain undisturbed. The Scriptorium has every tool necessary for the crafting of a perfect Chronicle except inspiration.

Pacing around the cavernous room, I cringe as my footsteps echo against the icy walls. I pass quarter bells in a state of worry that I may never arrive at the proper Chronicle for the *Genesis*. Theo peeks in from time for time, but otherwise I am without company. And ideas.

It is frigid in here, colder even than in the Conservation Chamber, which requires lower-than-usual temperatures for preservation. I tell myself that the glacial air is stymieing my writing. I summon an Attendant to fetch my sealskin cloak from the front hallway. Trying to stave off the bone chill, I walk in circles until the Attendant returns. I then wrap myself in the warmth of the cloak that kept me snug even in the Tundra.

Somewhat thawed, I fight to convince myself that I'm able to think again. I play with the idea of picking up where Madeline's Chronicle left off, vindicating her theories about the suspicious placement of the Tech with all my newfound knowledge. I toy with a Chronicle told from the point of view of the Techs' owners—the Founders—but I am repulsed by the thought of placing myself in their shoes. I even consider going the traditional route, uncovering the Relics as I found them in situ and disclosing my revelations about them as they came to me.

I reject them all. None will suffice. Because although I am writing something that will likely never be read on Founders' Day, it still must pass muster of the Archons when I read it aloud to them beforehand.

Only then does the solution dawn on me.

What if I wrote a Chronicle that could test the listener? In other words, what if I wrote something that would only resonate with someone who was aware that The Lex was man-made and not Gods-made? If I tread carefully, I could reveal a knowledge of the falsity imbedded into the Triad and New North without actually disclosing the truth about the Founders' intentional flooding of His Earth. And if I could read this Chronicle aloud to the Archons before Founders' Day, thereby testing the knowledge of those most likely to know at least some of the truth, I might be able to avoid the public revelation planned by Lukas. An overhaul of New North, despite Lukas's zealotry, has never been my objective. I must remind myself of that. In the end, exposing my twin's murderer is all that matters. Whatever greater good can come of that will be a blessing.

Besides, if I am honest with myself, I must admit certain truths, namely that there are so many wondrous elements of life in New North, and the Triad endeavors to provide for all of us survivors. None of us Aerie go without. Nor do the Boundary who depend on us. We have everything we need, except freedom.

So my decision is made. I will write the Chronicle in the style of the *Genesis* tale. Those Archons who know the truth about The Lex may well have been responsible for the death of Eamon. I am almost certain that they are. No other possible scenario makes sense.

I allow myself a bitter smile, thinking of the guilty parties, whoever they may be, walking directly into my trap. Archons, or any members of the Triad, really, consider themselves untouchable. Wrapping my cloak tightly around myself, my fingers brush up against the Triad symbol stitched on the front. Instead of the smooth embroidery of my Lady Mother, I feel a rent in the sealskin. I pull the cloak off my shoulders to examine it.

The tear is no accidental rip. Someone's knife tore through the Triad symbol, and the Triad symbol alone, in a clean cut. Not unlike the damage done to my gear the first night of the *Genesis* dig.

My jaw tightens. So I've been issued another warning. But this time I feel no fear, only icy resolve.

XXXX.

Augustus 15
Year 242, A.H.

The Archons assemble in the entry Hall. I line up at the end, as usual.

In the days since I've made my decision, my courage has faltered. Now I'm so nervous, I nearly knock down Pierre, the Archon closest to me. Although Theo has assured me that the Chronicle is perfect, I feel creeping panic. I aim to provoke a reaction from those Archons less oblivious to the truth than Theo—but now I'm uncertain what that reaction may be. Even my father won't be able to protect me if the guilty parties become violent. Which seems a distinct possibility, as the person responsible for the warnings I've received is certainly among the Archons.

"Hail Mother," my father intones, leading us in prayer.

I watch him, but I'm not listening to his words. In the days since I read his Chronicle, I can't look at him as I had before. I can't accept his fatherly affection or his Chief Archon instructions without skepticism. After all, he won the Archon Laurels and the Chief Archon role on the strength of a Chronicle that condemned Madeline as weak and sinful and incapable of Testing—she along with all women. What does he really think of me?

Yet even though I'm furious with my father for his true views on Maidens and Ladies, in spite of allowing me to train as Archon, I could never believe him to be complicit in the death of his own son. Eamon was as precious to him as he was to me. So I expect no unusual reaction from him, other than perhaps bafflement, when I read my Chronicle. From the others—like Laurence . . . What am I looking for in their faces? Something subtle like a raised eyebrow? Or will it be something obvious like a mouth opened, then quickly closed in a suppressed cry?

"Praise to the Gods," we chant in unison at the end of the prayer. I take a deep breath; I know what's coming.

My father turns his gaze to me. "Archon Eva, please read aloud your Chronicle of the *Genesis* excavation."

Walking down the long line of rigid, seemingly obedient Archons, my heart beats faster with every step, and my forehead beads with sweat despite the cold air. Last night, I memorized the Chronicle. That way, I could be certain that I'd be able to focus on reading the Archons' faces rather than the next lines. I take my position next to my father, square my shoulders, and begin.

"In the beginning, the Gods created the heavens and His Earth. After forming the seas and plants and trees and living creatures, the Gods decided to make a man in Their image. They named him Adam. The Gods then planted the Garden of Eden in the East, caused Her Sun to shine upon it, and placed the man They had formed in the garden to care for it."

I take a deep breath, scouring the Archons' faces for a flicker of recognition at the name Adam. But they are as cold and impassive as always.

"The Gods said to the man, 'You are free to eat from any tree in the garden, but you must not eat from the tree of the knowledge of good and evil, because if you do, you will certainly die.'

"The Gods watched the man and decided that it was not good for him to be lonely. They made a woman to be his companion. They named her Eve.

"But Adam and Eve were not alone. An evil being lived in this land with them, and he alone controlled the serpent, a craftier animal than any of the wild animals the Gods had made. One day, when Eve was apart from Adam and by herself, the serpent slithered over to her and asked, 'Did the Gods really say that you cannot eat from the tree of knowledge?'

"Eve answered, 'The Gods said that we would die if we ate from that tree.'

"The serpent said, 'You will not die. The Gods know that if you eat from the tree of knowledge, your eyes will be opened, and you will be like the Gods—knowing good from evil. That is why They do not want you to eat from it.'

"Eve looked at the beautiful apples hanging from the tree of knowledge and believed that they were not only good for food but also for gaining wisdom. So she picked an apple off the tree and took a bite from it. She walked over to Adam and offered the apple to him. And he took a bite from the apple as well.

"In that tick, their eyes were opened, and evil entered the world.

"The Gods asked them, 'Have you eaten from the tree we commanded you not to eat from?'

"When they answered truthfully, the Gods said, 'Mankind has now become like the Gods, knowing good from evil. Mankind must not be allowed to eat from the tree of life that is also here in the Garden of Eden and live forever.' The Gods banished the humans from the Garden of Eden, driving them out to harsh lands and guarding against mankind's return to the Garden of Eden with flaming swords.

"There in the bleak world beyond the Garden, the evil being revealed himself as the false god Apple. He took hold of Adam, Eve, and their progeny. The Gods gave mankind many chances to return to the worship of Them, but mankind believed itself to be like the Gods and persisted in its reverence of the false god Apple. When the Gods could stand it no more, They rained down the Healing upon mankind.

"Only then, when the Founders stood onboard the deck of the *Genesis*, did they see Apple's true nature—a false and evil creature. Not until that tick did mankind finally reject him. Slashing Apple's symbol from the worship tablets they had brought on board the *Genesis*, the Founders began to draft The Lex, the rightful history of the true Gods and the goodly abundance of laws which mankind must follow lest it ruin its second chance. And in this way, New North became the new Garden of Eden."

Once again I watch their faces. My father wears a minuscule smile, the one that surfaces when he's bemused at my mother's Ladyness but doesn't want her to know. No one other than me would even notice it. He is pleased with my Chronicle, nothing more, no matter his insensitivities toward women.

Theo's face bears a broad grin. He isn't bothering to hide his delight; it's the pleasure of a teacher at his star pupil. I have to stop myself from smiling back.

The other Archons' faces haven't changed since I've begun; they are one in their stoicism. Nothing readable, no hint of conspiracy—nothing at all, except in Laurence. But how should I read the rage I see flickering there? Is it just his everyday loathing of me? His usual hatred of Eva the Archon? Or is it his fear that I'll take his coveted Chief role when my father steps down? Whatever the source of his contempt, I don't see any recognition of my Chronicle's reference to the Biblical *Genesis*.

How is it possible that this entire arm of the Triad is ignorant of the truth? Did not a single one of them ever look at those books in the Vault? Maybe they couldn't make sense of those arcane texts without knowing what I know. But if Eamon's killer isn't standing here in these Halls, where will I find him? In the other arms of the Triad?

"Excellent, Archon Eva," my father says, breaking the silence. "With your Chronicle, you have captured well the importance of the Relics onboard the *Genesis*. In fact, you have explained well the significance of the *Genesis* itself." He pauses. Taking a moment to peer at each and every Archon individually, he adds, "If there are no objections, I believe that you are best suited to read aloud your Chronicle on Founders' Day."

I want to revel in his pride, but the words from his own Chronicle hold me back. So I simply nod in acceptance of his generous compliment. From the other Archons, there are smiles of agreement. Some of the smiles look genuine, while others appear strained. Yet no one dares object.

Except Archon Laurence.

Arms folded, shoulders back, he faces my father across the great Hall. "This Neophyte Archon, this"—he spits the word—"Maiden. You really think she is 'best suited to read aloud the Chronicle.'" He mocks my father's commanding voice.

Perhaps I hear a gasp from some of the others. I've stopped breathing. But my father remains calm even in the face of what can easily be interpreted as heresy and sedition. I feel a sudden rush of admiration for him, even the old love, in spite of his flaws. The Lex would give him the right to strike Laurence down. In that instant, I see the difference between a true leader and one who envies such intangible power. And alas, I am certain I fall into the latter category, despite Lukas's insistence to the contrary. It almost brings me a measure of peace.

"Yes, I do, Archon Laurence," my father says evenly. "She wrote the Chronicle, and she is the appropriate one to read it to the people of New North."

The words only serve to further incense Laurence. "The *Genesis* is my Site. I found mention of it in the archives, I discovered that the Site had reopened, and I'm the one that led the dig. No mere girl should get the credit. No mere daughter. The glory should go to me."

With the same steady voice and a hand on the hilt of the

sword at his side, my father replies, "The *Genesis* belongs to New North, not you. As does the glory. And the decision as to who should present the Chronicle of the *Genesis* belongs to me. I choose Archon Eva."

XXXXI.

Augustus 15
Year 242, A.H.

As Lukas and I make one last trip through the Hall of Archons, my thoughts aren't on what we might find but the fight over my Chronicle. Laurence is more unpredictable—and therefore dangerous—than I'd realized. This new worry fuels my concerns over finding Eamon's killer. Is my father's life in danger as well? I'd argued against another trip to the Hall after our narrow escape last time; I didn't think we'd uncover anything new, and indeed our limited bells there yield nothing fresh, but Lukas was insistent and persuasive.

After a mercifully safe exit, we return to Lukas's chamber in the Clothing Keep to finalize our Founders' Day arrangements. His room feels impossibly warm after the bitter chill outside. I peel off my hat, gloves, and coat and watch as Lukas removes his outer furs. He wears nothing but a thin tunic over leggings, and the tunic clings to his chest and arms. For a tick, we stare at each other. Even though I'm hot, I once again crave the warmth of Lukas's arms. He reaches out to me, and I turn my face up to his. Waiting for his kiss, just like last time.

Instead, Lukas hands me a bound volume.

Blushing, I turn my attention to it. Is this some sort of present? I'm nervous about opening it at first; the last time he gave me a book, it was Eamon's secret journal. I don't think I could handle another shock like that. But the ticks are short until the Founders' Day ceremony starts tomorrow morning.

"What is this?" I ask.

"It's your speech for tomorrow," he says, as if that explains everything.

I look at him, confused. "My speech for tomorrow is already written; you know that. I'll be reading my Chronicle to the entire population of New North. Just like you wanted." I don't go into the awful fight between my father and Archon Laurence over who would read my Chronicle on Founders' Day. I didn't want to relive the experience and in the process give Lukas one more thing to worry about.

"This is something for you to read after your Chronicle. I think it's the best way to sway the people of New North to side with us." His tone is matter-of-fact, as if we've already agreed upon this.

"Side with us?" I repeat.

His face is as inscrutable as the Archons'. "Yes. Side with us in making changes to New North. Peaceably."

I gape at him. "Why wouldn't tomorrow be peaceable?"

"Eva, I believe that you are the only one who can persuade the people to change; that's why you are the *Angakkuq*. I don't want to use force. No one does. War is not the answer. You know it. We know it. There are far too few people left on this earth to risk a single life."

His words have the intended effect; they reassure me.

But as I skim through the text, throughout which Latin words are sprinkled, the reassurance turns to grave concern. Here is the real history of New North as we've uncovered these past few weeks. No detail is spared, from the Founders' intentional flooding of the earth, to their creation of The Lex, and the falsity of the Gods found in the pages of The Lex. Even the actual documents upon which the Founders based their fabrications are mentioned: the Bible, myths, and legends.

I don't think the people can bear this, and it is precisely the revelation of this entire truth I'd hoped to avoid by sharing my Chronicle instead. I have explained all this to Lukas, how we could identify those with knowledge, the New North wrongdoers, by simply reading my Chronicle aloud. We could then take action and perhaps even create the change he longs for quietly and without alarming the people.

I thought he had agreed with me. I obviously mistook silence for acquiescence.

There is something very wrong with this speech, and it's not just the content. Lukas led me to believe that only he and I know the full truth, that his Boundary comrades know only that the *Angakkuq* is working to support their general beliefs. But someone else had to have created this, someone who'd been told everything.

"Who wrote this?" I demand.

"I did."

I shake my head. "Come on, Lukas. There's Latin in here."

"I wrote it, Eva. Why is that so hard to believe?" He looks offended.

"You know Latin? Don't deceive me."

"Yes."

"But you said you didn't read Eamon's journal because it was in Latin. You had me read it to you."

He shrugs, his bottomless black eyes unwavering. "That's what you assumed when I asked you to read it to me. I simply did not want to invade his private thoughts without your permission."

I don't know why this explanation troubles me so, but I am unnerved. Does he think he can so easily sway me? That he can just hand me a script and I'll present it to the entire population of New North like some sort of puppet? We have never discussed anything other than finding Eamon's killer and identifying those within the Triad who know the truth about New North—and only then, if all goes according to plan, maybe making some kinds of changes behind the scenes. Beyond that, we really haven't formulated or discussed a single course of action. I might indeed agree with his approach, but I deserve to be consulted before decisions are made. Especially if I'm his precious *Angakkuq*.

A fight is brewing between us, and I'm just about to launch into it when I hear a knock at the door. I glance over at Lukas. The Clothing Keeper at this bell? Lukas reaches for my outerwear and leads me to the window. He's right to get me out of here. It doesn't really matter who it is; I cannot be found in an Attendant's chamber tonight of all nights.

Lukas pushes aside the heavy skins covering the opening. If I'm quiet and quick enough, I might slip out unnoticed while he speaks to the person at the door. I grab my gear and ready myself to climb out the window when I spot them. A line of guards from the Hall of Archons standing outside Lukas's chamber.

Lukas drops the skins.

What are we going to do now? Tears of frustration stream down my face. We are so close to finding out who killed Eamon and finding out the truth—and now we never will.

A voice calls out from behind the front door. "You can come out. Or I can come in."

Is there any choice? We know what's waiting outside. But is the alternative really any better? *The gallows,* I think, remembering that pour soul who was put to death as a warning to me. Was there ever really any other possible ending to this prolonged subterfuge? No, the gallows awaited me from the moment I decided to take avenging my brother's death into my own hands.

Lukas opens the door. It's Archon Theo.

XXXXII.

Augustus 15
Year 242, A.H.

Theo? Of all the Archons to be involved in this terrible conspiracy to suppress the truth, Theo is the last one I'd suspect.

"Archon Eva, are you all right?" he asks. He looks and sounds shocked at my presence in Lukas's chambers and concerned for my well-being. How did he not know I was in here?

Did he follow us from the Hall of Archons? Does he think that I'm here against my will? That maybe I'm Lukas's prisoner? My mind squirms with questions, and my survival instincts tell me to play the victim, but I can't do that to Lukas. He'd get the gallows for certain. I've got to try something else.

Theo turns to Lukas with an expression as menacing as he can muster. "Did you hurt her?"

I place a hand on Lukas's shoulder. "I'm fine, Archon Theo. Truly."

His eyes widen, and he steps away from us; it's unimaginable to him that an Archon and daughter of the Aerie would willingly touch the shoulder of a Boundary boy. "What in the Gods are you doing in here, Eva? In . . . in an Attendant's chamber?" His confusion is so strong that he can barely stammer out the words.

"This is Lukas," I reply, forcing him to meet my gaze. "He was my brother's Companion. I wanted to talk with him about Eamon."

Theo's eyes narrow. He will not be easily deceived. "That explanation strains credulity, Eva. A Maiden venturing out after the final bell to chat with a Boundary Companion about her dead brother?"

I have to hand it to him: He is nothing if not logical. I lower my head humbly, as if beseeching his understanding. Even his forgiveness. "It's true, Archon Theo."

I wonder if he suspects that Lukas and I are more than master and servant. I doubt it; every member of the Triad has witnessed my genuine affection for Jasper. I feel that all-too-familiar pang of guilt. Does the very thought of a Maiden and a Boundary together alone so offend Theo?

"Is that what you two were doing sneaking around the Hall of Archons tonight?" Theo demands. "Chatting about your dead brother?"

By the Gods, Theo saw us there. He followed us from the Hall to Lukas's chambers. He knew that someone had broken into the Hall of Archon after-bells with a Boundary person in tow, but he had no idea that it was me. The

Archon uniform must have masked my identity; it's truly uniform in every sense of the word, after all. No wonder he is so shocked and disappointed to see *me* of all people here. His favorite pupil deceived him. Not only that; I've violated The Lex countless times along the way, an anathema to Theo. My near word-for-word knowledge of The Lex was what endeared me to him in the first place; I was one of the few who could interpret and bend it.

He shakes his head in fury and disbelief. "I knew someone was examining the *Genesis* Tech in the Conservation Chamber at night. It was never precisely where I left it. I thought it was my brother . . . I was certain Laurence was warning you further, trying to sabotage our efforts because of his dislike and fear of you. But I never dreamed that *you* were the one breaking into the Chamber. Never you. Why did you do it, Eva?"

"You say 'warning me further,'" I reply. "Was it Laurence who broke into my *iglu* and stabbed that awful knife through my clothing?"

Theo bows his head.

I could offer other excuses to him, but what is the point? We have both been hiding truths from each other. And unless I tell Theo every piece of the secret history we've uncovered—which he may or may not believe—nothing will justify my many Lex violations tonight. But what can he say of the truth he withheld from me?

"What are you going to do?" I ask.

He looks sad. Pleas that prey on his own withholding of truth will not move him. All that remains is our punishment.

"You've left me with only one choice. I've got to turn you over to the Lexors for judgment. I will pray to the Gods that you're sentenced only to banishment." My hand still rests on Lukas's shoulder, but I feel him shift slightly. He knows what's coming. He doesn't even register for Theo beyond his certain fate at the gallows.

Theo turns away from us and heads toward the door. In a tick, he will summon the guards. All that Lukas and I have worked so hard to discover will be lost, like *natquik*, snow that drifts away in a strong wind.

Before Theo's hand touches the door handle, Lukas grabs him. He pulls Theo in front of him, wraps one arm around Theo's body, and uses the other to place the blade of his *pana* under Theo's chin. My heart leaps into my throat.

"No!" I hear myself gasp. Even though I desperately want to escape from this situation, I don't want it to come at the cost of Theo's life. "Don't hurt him, Lukas," I beg, my voice trembling.

Theo's eyes are wide with terror.

"Eva," says Lukas, "*we're* the ones left with only one choice. This old man has said so himself."

A hot tear falls from my lashes. "There's always a choice."

Lukas presses his blade against Theo's neck. Theo stiffens, his belly jutting out, his arm twisted behind his back. "I've been raised for this my whole life, Eva," Lukas hisses. "Find the *Angakkuq*. Place the *Angakkuq* in motion. Uncover the truth. Set New North free. I've made so many sacrifices to reach that goal, and we are so close . . . I can't let this Archon go."

Theo stares at me. Maybe he's given up. Now I can see nothing in his weary, wrinkled eyes other than resigned exhaustion.

"We can find a way to tell people the truth without hurting him," I say, stepping a little closer to Lukas and Theo with each word.

"If we let him leave here, you and I will be swinging from the gallows. We are going to get you back home without anyone finding out about this." Lukas tries to sound convincing, but his voice wavers. I know in that tick he doesn't want to kill Theo, either.

"Lukas, please don't." I am crying now, but I feel no shame. "Eamon wouldn't have wanted anyone else to die for the truth."

"Eamon." At the mention of Eamon's name, tears start to stream down Lukas's face as well. "I thought your brother was the *Angakkuq*. But it was you. It could only ever be you. And I had to make certain that it was you."

I finally understand. The sacrifices that Lukas refers to can only mean one thing: Eamon.

I back away, horror creeping in with the revelation. "No, no, no, no. It can't be you. Tell me you aren't the one who killed Eamon."

Lukas doesn't deny me. He chokes on his words. "Eamon wasn't the *Angakkuq*; you are. He could not have accomplished what you have with your Chronicles, and he could not have rallied the people the way you have and will again tomorrow. Believe me, Eva, I didn't want to do what I had to do. I loved Eamon like a brother, but there was no other course."

"Loved him? You killed him!"

He sighs, his grip on Theo slackening just a bit. "I did love him. I do love him. I did a terrible thing. For the greater good."

I back into the corner of the chamber, as far as I can get

from my brother's murderer. "You are no better than the Founders who drowned billions to create a new world!"

He nods sadly. "I suppose it's fitting punishment. To know that I love you—not just admire your greatness as the *Angakkuq* but truly love you—just as I tell you the one thing which will ensure that you'll never love me back."

He drops the *pana* knife and releases Theo. "Goodbye, Eva."

Theo and I both collapse as he vanishes into the night. The *pana* clatters to the floor.

I'm not sure how much time passes after that. A tick, a bell, a lifetime. I am lost and adrift in this tiny room until Theo pulls me back into the present.

"Eva, I have to order the Guards to go after Lukas," he grunts, pushing himself to his feet and leaning over to help me up. "We can't let the murderer of your brother go free."

He doesn't need to convince me. All these many, many *siniks* searching for my brother's killer, and he was standing by my side the whole time. It's unbearable.

He pulls back the window covering and calls out orders to the Guards. Then he turns back to me. "I'm so sorry, Eva, but I must turn you over to them as well. The Lex demands it."

I shake my head. No, not this. Not now. Not with the horror of Eamon's death looming before me. "Please, Theo. Please don't."

"The tragedy of your brother's murder doesn't excuse your actions," Theo states plainly.

He's right. How can I expect leniency simply by begging for it? I owe Theo more. I can't expect him to take a leap of faith when I haven't taken one myself. Through my tears, I say, "What if I told you that Lukas and I were in the

Hall of Archons because the *Genesis* Tech revealed something terrible about the creation of New North?"

He sighs, again looking more resigned than angry. "What do you mean?"

"Archon Theo, Tech is not an altar where pre-Healing people worshipped Apple. Tech was a way that pre-Healing people communicated with one another . . . and did all sorts of other extraordinary things. Apple was not a false god to whom they prayed; Apple was the Keep that made the Tech."

Now I have his attention. He straightens. "That can't be true."

"It is. I can take you back to the Hall of Archons and show you." I consider which of the many nightmarish facts to tell him. "Listen to me, and listen well: The Healing was no act of retribution by the Gods. The Founders themselves flooded the earth."

"Come on, Eva. Do you think a preposterous lie—"

"It's true!" I shout. "If you find what I'm saying to be a lie, then I will go to the gallows willingly. The Founders perverted the truth! They took Tech, and they took the Bible, and they took—"

"Stop." Now it's his turn to interrupt. He moves closer to the door. "That one word. Say it again."

I know the one he means. "Bible."

"Yes. Where did you learn that word?"

"Lukas and . . . I found parts of the Bible stored in the Tech and elsewhere and compared them to The Lex." I almost mention Jasper's name, but if I am to die, I want to spare him. He never asked for this. "Several sections are nearly identical."

"What is the Bible?" Theo asks.

The question catches me off guard. He honestly doesn't know; he's asking me because he's curious. "It's the religious document from before the Healing."

He shifts on his feet. "I've seen that word mentioned in certain Relics. I've kept private tabs on it over the years. But I've never heard anyone mention it before; it doesn't seem to be on the Triad's mind." He moves away from the door. "Okay. I sense truth within you, and I will consider letting you go for now, Eva—if you answer one question for me."

"Anything."

"Why did you break all these laws, Eva? What made you do it?"

"Because my brother was seeking the truth about New North when he . . ." I can't bring myself to finish the sentence. I wipe my eyes and plow forward. "I wanted to finish what he started. Becoming a Testor was only part of that; finding the facts about the pre-Healing world, the creation of New North and the writing of The Lex were the other parts. Now that I've pieced together the past, I believe that he would want me to share that truth with New North."

"You are planning on making your revelation tomorrow, then?" He understands now.

"Yes. At the Founders' Day celebration."

His brow furrows. "Eva, what is an *Angakkuq*?" He butchers the word, but I know what he's asking.

I take a deep breath and answer, "The Boundary believe that the *Angakkuq* is a spiritual person, a sort of shaman who can serve the higher powers by bringing about order to the world."

"Your friend Lukas . . . the Boundary people . . . they believe you are this *Angakkuq*?"

I feel sick. "I've explained that I'm only a Maiden in search of the answers."

He pauses for a long tick. "I won't turn you over to the guards. If you do not get the reaction you seek after you speak tomorrow, the Triad will exact punishment enough."

Without thinking, I leap forward and swoop him into an embrace. "Thank you," I breathe.

He's clearly uncomfortable being so close to me. As he wriggles free, he asks, "Where can I find you to report on Lukas? You deserve to know when we find him."

"At Jasper's home. I need to tell him everything, too. Before tomorrow."

"His parents will let you in at this bell?"

"I'll scale the walls to talk with him privately."

"Your skill with climbing comes as much in handy as your skill with words, it seems." His tone is lighter now. Perhaps he, too, is relieved—or at least relieved at having an excuse not to send me to my death.

I try to smile at him, but tears course down my cheeks instead. The kindness and trust he's granted me, contrasted with the evil and deception perpetrated by Lukas, are a welcome gift. "Thank you, Theo."

He grants me a guarded smile, then turns toward the door. "I'll handle the guards. You go your own way. And Eva? Tighten that sash around your cloak. It's frigid out there."

XXXXIII.

Augustus 15
Year 242, A.H.

I tap Jasper on the shoulder. He doesn't even move, he's so deeply asleep. A sliver of moonlight illuminates his face—the only part of him I can see, given that he's laden with the bedcovers of a high-ranking Gallant and Lexor—and I realize that I've never seen him sleep before. This is the sight to which I will awaken every morning after our Union.

Our Union.

Will that even happen after I give my speech tomorrow? Will this be the only time I'll ever see him this way? I know my brother made the ultimate sacrifice for New North. If I must make a sacrifice, too, so be it. My only regret is that I wasted any ticks or feelings on my brother's killer.

Sweet Jasper. I study the curve of his jaw and his angular cheek bones. His lashes are surprisingly long, almost like a Maiden's. Without the usual Gallant styling, his hair is curly and longer than I thought, nearly to his shoulder. I stroke a lock that loops around his collarbone. He is beautiful.

Jasper would have never hurt Eamon. How could I have ever suspected him? How could I have ever betrayed him by kissing Lukas, my brother's killer?

I run my fingers along Jasper's cheek. He makes a small noise, almost like a moan. Although his eyelids are still closed, his fingers creep out from the bedcovers and cover mine. He pulls me down onto the bed, and his eyes flutter open.

"Eva!" He looks so shocked that I realize he must have been dreaming when he reached for me. "What in the Gods are you doing here?"

"Shhh." I place a single finger over his lips. "I'm sorry to frighten you."

"I'm happy to see you," he says underneath my finger. "This is just unorthodox."

"I wish this was a simple visit."

"What's wrong? You wouldn't scale the walls unless it was serious." He grins mischievously. "Even though I am irresistible."

"I'm here to tell you the truth."

Jasper's eyebrows knit in concern, and his smile vanishes. "About what?"

Does he worry that my revelation has something to do with our Union? I wouldn't be surprised, given how strangely our Betrothal path began. I reach for his hand to reassure him, squeeze it tightly.

"Not about us, Jasper. About everything else."

I'm not certain how to begin, but once I start, the words

pour out of me in torrents. I tell him nearly everything I've uncovered, starting with the Testing. Elizabet's Relics and Lukas's ability to read her Tech. The reality of the Boundary lands and people. The origins of The Lex in the pre-Healing Bible. The actual nature of Tech and Apple. Madeline's journal and the *Genesis*. Even the secret found on the *Genesis* about the Founders' intentional flooding of the earth. The only thing I don't share is Eamon's murder and Lukas's betrayal. Not yet, and I'm not sure why.

I grow quiet, and so does Jasper. His hands slide out of mine.

I wonder what he's thinking. Can he ever trust me again after all the secrets I've kept from him? After all this time that I've spent alone with another man, a Boundary at that. A dark shadow falls over his golden profile. I could ascribe it to the moon's movement, but I know well its source. The horror of the truth. Maybe the horror of my involvement in unearthing that truth, too.

And yet, amidst it all, I see a spark of hope on his face. A glimmer of Jasper the Gallant returns. "The Triad. We've got to report this to the Triad."

At first, I'm just thrilled that his initial reaction isn't akin to Theo's: confusion, then anger, then resignation. But still I realize that I face enormous problems with his suggestion. He thinks that the Triad can fix this problem. I only have a few ticks to explain why going to the Triad isn't possible. And to make him understand why it's so important to challenge everything he's held dear about the Aerie.

"What if I told you that I think the Triad already knows? Some of them, anyway. And that they've intentionally kept the truth from the New North people to make sure we stay in the roles they've prescribed for us?" I speak with confidence, even though I don't have actual proof of the Triad's awareness; my belief has always been more intuitive than that.

He recoils. I knew this would be hard for him. He has family members and friends in the Triad. Just like me.

"No, Eva. The Triad? Maybe the early Triad members who were also Founders, but not the Triad members today. Why would you ever think that?"

Since I don't have proof, I explain to him about the acts of hatred toward me, about the violent and unambiguous warnings. And Eamon. I know that the animosity toward me can be justified by the dislike of a Maiden in an Archon's role, but the same can't be said for Eamon. I tell him about Eamon's death, although I leave out the part about Lukas. Why I am protecting my brother's killer? Part of me loathes myself for the omission, but another part is starting to understand that I have to keep Lukas's image clean, or Jasper might challenge our discoveries.

"No, Eva. Not Eamon."

"Yes, Jasper. Eamon. And even if the Triad doesn't know, and even if they're not responsible for Eamon's death, my gut tells me that they will block me from trying to share the truth with the people of New North. It will jeopardize the Triad's control."

"Surely you don't mean your father? Or my uncle?"

"I don't think so, but I've been wrong about so many things."

Jasper rolls away from me to stare at the blank wall beside his bed. I sit quietly for a few ticks on the edge farthest away from him, hoping that a little space is all that's needed to sway him. I know I'm asking a tremendous amount. I've had several months to deal with this deluge of truth; Jasper doesn't have that luxury. He needs to process it now. Theo will be here shortly, and I need Jasper's allegiance.

I say his name a few times.

Nothing.

I've never known him to ignore me; such unGallantry goes against all his beliefs. Can he hear me? Or did he become engulfed somewhere in the avalanche of information?

I have an idea. "Do you remember what you said when I asked you to search inside the Lexors' Vault for documents about the *Genesis*?"

He doesn't answer. He doesn't even glance over at me.

I supply the answer for him. "You said, 'The people of New North deserve the truth about the Healing, The Lex, everything. If we've been lied to by our Founders, we need to discover the deception and tell the truth.'"

Still nothing. I'm desperate.

Moving around to his side of the bed, I kneel before him. "If we go to the Triad first and tell them what I've learned, I will get the gallows. I have violated The Lex so many times to gain that information, even if the Triad wasn't trying to shut me up, they would have no choice but to punish me. I am trusting you with all that I've done in the name of the truth, and praying to whatever Gods exist that you will help me. The people deserve to know. I need to know that you have my back when I'm up on that dais tomorrow, Jasper."

Finally he turns from the wall and looks at me. His eyes are a startling blue even in this darkness. "I want to, Eva," he says. "I love you, and I don't believe that you would ever lie to me. But this is hard. Whether your accusations about The Lex and the Founders are true or not, I still believe our world is a good one. I love New North. The Triad makes sure that everyone has what they need, and everyone's virtue is protected. Not like the pre-Healing world. Why would I want to upset the order in our society after all that mankind has been through? It's not like we have anywhere else to go."

"I understand, Jasper." He's not going to help me. It was always a gamble. I stand, though my knees quake. I've got to be brave, because tomorrow I'll be out there all alone.

Turning to leave, I hear Jasper's voice. "But you're right about what I said before. If there are lies about New North—its present or its past—we must root them out and show them to the people. And root out the liars, too. Only then can a just society be restored." He pauses for a tick and says, "I'll help you, Eva."

Did he really just say that? I whirl and face him. "You'll stand behind me tomorrow when I announce the truth at the Founders' Day celebration?"

"I will."

I'm not sure he can stand it, but he needs to know that in addition to the Triad, Lukas might be a threat. That we must be prepared physically as well as emotionally for tomorrow's revelations. "One more thing, Jasper. Lukas and I had a falling-out today. He wants change in New North—including a breakdown of this barrier between Boundary and Aerie—and I'm not sure he'll stop at my speech."

"What do you mean?"

"I mean, if he doesn't get the reaction he wants from the people after my speech, he might use force."

My Betrothed nods. "Then we will be prepared for that."
Jasper the Gallant has returned.

I hadn't even noticed, but I've moved closer to him. Very
close. We lean toward each other. Our lips touch tenderly,
almost sadly. We cling to each other, together on the only
life raft left in rising flood waters.

XXXXIV.

Augustus 16
Year 242, A.H.

Standing on the roof of Jasper's home, I prepare to descend. Just as I'm about to throw a line over the edge, the view of New North, glistening and peaceful in the partial moonlight, stops me. Could Jasper be right? Would my revelation force the people to sacrifice a society that's largely good for the sake of past truths? Yet how can I abandon my path now? No, I must continue.

I slide down my line to the ground. Theo isn't here yet. What's keeping him? Have they found Lukas? I'd be surprised if the plodding, loud Archon-Guards could track a silent, expert hunter and climber like Lukas. Still, I shudder at the thought of standing face-to-face again with Eamon's killer, a person I thought was my friend and maybe more.

But the thought of Lukas's imprisonment gives me

pause. If he's locked within the Aerie jails and subjected to the torture rumored to happen there, will he divulge everything? Including my participation? I can't believe that the Triad would let me deliver my Chronicle tomorrow with such accusations hanging in the air.

Pursuing Lukas right now would ruin my chance to mount that dais tomorrow and lift the blinders off New North's eyes. A chance that may never come again. Should I really jettison the opportunity to tell New North the truth—an act my brother would have willingly died for—because of my fury at Lukas? My need for immediate revenge?

I hear Theo's lumbering footsteps approach, and I make an impossible decision. I will exact my revenge on Lukas another time—of that I will make certain. I can't sacrifice my only chance for change, because it would be unfair to Eamon. He *died* for truth.

"I'm so sorry, Eva," Theo says, breathless from exertion. "We lost Lukas's trail before we even got close to the Ring."

"Don't blame yourself, Theo. Lukas is gifted in tracking and the ways of snow. If he doesn't want us to find him, he won't be found." I don't mention that having been trained by Lukas myself, I might be the only one who can find him now.

"I promise you that at dawn, we will cross over into the Boundary. We will not stop searching until we find him."

Facing Theo square on, I ask, "Do you trust me?"

His sad expression resurfaces. "Before tonight I did. Now I'm not sure. I want to believe in you and the things you told me, even though they were so incredible, so awful. But I don't think you could make them up."

"Can you believe in me enough to call off the Guards? Tell them you made a mistake."

This is no small deed I ask of him. Repercussions will certainly follow for dragging the Hall of Archons Guards out after the final bell on a whim. On a search mission at that. Probably at the hand of his brother.

"Why would you want me to do that?"

"Once you find Lukas, my involvement in this will come out. The Triad will never let me mount that stage tomorrow. I need to make sure I read my Chronicle at the Founders' Day celebration. Then I want to kill Lukas myself."

Theo stares at me long and hard. "I'll do it, Eva. Not just for you and Eamon. For New North."

XXXXV.

Augustus 16
Year 242, A.H.

I've never been so nervous. Not when I passed under the Gate in the Ring and left behind the Aerie for the first time. Not when I first stared down into the bottomless crevasse where I uncovered Elizabet's Relics in the Testing. Not when I stole into the Hall of Archons under the cover of darkness. No, this moment is more terrifying than any other, because this is the tick that will determine whether all the risk and all the sacrifice were worthwhile. I could change everything.

My fellow Archons and I stand shoulder to shoulder on the Aerie town square dais the morning of the Founders' Day celebration. We serve as the black, sealskin-suited backdrop for the Triad leaders—my father as the Chief Archon, Jasper's Uncle Ian as the Chief Lexor, and Henry

as the Chief Basilikon. The flames of a hundred torches
frame us, though they're hard to make out in the brilliant
sunlight, and the entire population of New North serves as
our audience.

Squinting into the sun reflecting off the ice-crusted building of the town square, I review the scene. All the elements
are in place. The Triad flanks me, my sole ally Theo and
my nemesis Laurence among them, and the people stand
before me, a sea of eager eyes. The faces of those leaders I
need to assess are close enough to inspect, even though I'll
have to turn around to see them. Jasper and a few trusted
Gallant friends, kept in the dark except for the hint of some
unnamed amorphous threat, are in place throughout the
crowd to protect me, should Lukas surface.

I breathe deeply of the icy air. Maybe this gambit will
work, after all. Maybe I will transform the future and set
all of New North free with the simple words of the truth.
Maybe I can do what Eamon wanted. But "maybe" feels
like an enormous leap into an abyss deeper than any crevasse I've ever encountered.

I try to calm my nerves by listening to the Chief Basilikon's prayers; they used to soothe me. But now all I hear
embedded in those offerings are lies. Lies about the Founders, The Lex, and the Gods that do nothing for my mount-
ing apprehension. Lies that only serve to ratchet up my
anxiety for my task. I've got to stay focused.

Instead, I try to tune out the chanting and mentally
recite the speech I'll soon give. I'm so intent on drowning
out the words of the Chief Basilikon that I almost miss my
own summoning.

"Archon Eva, please join me." The Chief Basilikon
booms over the silent, prayerful New North crowd.

I march to the front of the dais with a confidence I don't feel. I stand just behind the Chief Basilikon, as befits my rank. The face of my mother beams up at me from the crowds, and I can almost hear her bragging to her friends, "Look at my beautiful Eva up there; I always knew she'd be the first Maiden-Archon." As if she had supported me all along.

I'm about to let her down. Crush her, actually.

My father takes his place alongside the Chief Basilikon and gestures to the crowd. "As you may have heard, the Gods have decided that it was time New North witness firsthand the bravery of our Founders. We Archons were recently blessed with the discovery of that most important of Relics—the very boat that brought our Founders to the shores of New North in the final days of the Healing. The *Genesis*."

The crowd erupts as if they've never heard the news, even though I'm certain that most have been gossiping about the *Genesis* since we returned from the dig. New North is a small place, and word travels from Keep to Keep and home to home faster than an arctic hare. Still, it wouldn't be seemly to admit their knowledge, and a subdued reception of the announcement would be just that.

Unable to contain his smile, my father glances over at me; his face is shining with pride. I feel sick to my stomach. No matter my recent uncertainties about my father, I love him.

He gestures for me to step forward. "I give you Archon Eva."

The crowd reaction to the news of the *Genesis* pales in comparison to the roar over me. My father's chest puffs up even higher, and I wonder how deflated he'll be after I finish my speech. Even now, it's hard to disappoint him.

The people begin to chant, "Eva, Eva, Eva." It continues until it becomes a roar overtaking all other sound. The people begin to toss items on the stage. At first, I instinctively duck, and I see the Guards call out in alarm. But then, when I see the objects—garlands, wreaths, and other treasures—I reach out to catch them and form a pile of their offerings next to my feet.

After the noise subsides, my father continues. "Her research led us to the exact Site of the *Genesis,* and she was the first Archon to cross the threshold. She deciphered the horror and the epiphanies of those days on the *Genesis,* helping us all understand the precise moment in which the Gods visited our Founders and gave them mankind's second chance at life through faith. I'm certain you won't be surprised that the Archons chose Archon Eva to write the Chronicle of this most important Relic." He and the Chief Basilikon step to the side to give me command of the dais.

I open my palms out to the people. My voice cracks as I try to assume the chanting tone used so effectively by the Basilikons to invoke The Lex. Because that's exactly how I want the people to hear my Chronicle and the words that follow—as a sacred text. "In the beginning, the Gods created the heavens and His Earth . . ."

I scan the crowd as I continue with my Chronicle version of the Biblical *Genesis.* All I see are accepting stares and nodding heads; the people look transfixed by the tale I tell. I don't see any expressions of recognition or hear any disconcerting sounds, even from the other Triad members. Until I reach my mother. She's heard the story of Adam and Eve before, I'm certain of it. I stare into her eyes as I continue almost automatically with my Chronicle. How in the Gods would my mother know the Bible? She of all people, follower of The Lex, perfect Lady, oblivious to the workings of New North beyond the hearth and home. I must be mistaken.

"Slashing Apple's symbol from the worship tablets they had brought on board the *Genesis*, the Founders began to draft The Lex   the goodly and rightful history of the true Gods and the laws which mankind must follow or ruin their second chance. And in this way, New North became the new Garden of Eden."

I finish with my Chronicle and pause before I begin the next phase of my speech. A long shadow falls across the dais, causing a break in the relentless sunlight. I glance up. Figures have begun to assemble on the ridge of the Ring.

From this distance, they look like dark outlines against the brightness of the sun and the blue sky. To the untrained eye, the shadows would cause no alarm; they could easily be Ring-Guards. Yet, I know better. From the outline of their *atlatl* and long *ipu* spears and the flap of their cloaks, I recognize them as Boundary.

Jasper sees me staring and follows my line of sight. He knows they are Boundary, too. Placing one hand on the hilt of his sword, he lifts the other; I know he's about to signal to his men. I make our agreed-upon "hold" gesture. I need one more tick to see if I can win the people over with my words before Lukas resorts to his weapons.

XXXXVI.

Augustus 16
Year 242, A.H.

"This Chronicle is a fiction we were led to believe was the truth," I yell out. I hope I'm loud enough for Lukas and his men on the Ring to hear me. I don't want violence before I get a shot at peace. "New North was founded on a lie."

Gasps and cries sound from the crowd, and the expressions of betrayal on the people's faces nearly send me into silence. In the tick before I will myself to continue, the Guards surrounding the stage assume a defensive position. Whether because of my words or the people's reactions, I don't know. Either way, I don't have much time before I get dragged off the stage.

"Eva," I hear my father call out from the stage behind

me, his voice full of alarm and anger. Only a few ticks before my period of grace ends.

"The pre-Healing world is not as we think, and the Healing is not as we've been told. The pre-Healing people were sinful and corrupt, but no more than we. They worshipped a God not unlike our Gods, and in fact, our Lex is not divinely inspired but instead modeled on the pre-Healing religious text, the Bible, as well as other long-existing myths and legends. The so-called false god Apple is merely a Keep that created the pre-Healing Tech. Tech isn't evil, just a fancy means of communicating. Not unlike our hawks. In fact, the most sinful act of the pre-Healing people—and the deed most deserving of divine punishment—is the one undertaken by the Founders themselves. The intentional flooding of our Earth—"

"That's enough!" Chief Lexor Ian cries out, as he steps forward and slaps me across the face. I skid across the dais floor, blood pouring from my nose.

"How dare you!" he continues, drawing ever closer to my bloody face as I scuttle backward across the stage. "The Founders didn't submerge the Earth; they just finished the job that the pre-Healing people had already started. By the time of the Healing, mankind's machines had already polluted the sky with as much heat as thousands of nuclear bombs. The oceans were already rising. The flood waters were inevitable. Destruction was coming. The Founders simply made sure that the final submersion happened in such a way that mankind could continue on, living in a way that is good and true. The Founders were heroes, not murderers."

As my father pulls Ian away from me, Laurence races to join Ian's side. Laurence and Ian in alignment? The allegiances are now clear. This answers many of my questions about the small acts of violence against me and the horrific gallows message.

Laurence and Ian face off against my father, and silence fills the Aerie Town square, becoming a presence unto itself. By uttering those words in defense of the Founders, Ian did more damage to their legacy than I could have ever done alone. He has confirmed that I speak the truth.

I struggle to stand, slipping on planking made slick with my blood.

Laurence turns and raises his hand to strike me—I guess he wants his chance to vent his rage, too—but my father grabs his arm before he makes contact.

"What Eva says is true. Isn't it?" my father asks both of them. He wants the people to hear the truth very clearly.

"Yes," Ian answers. "We should be celebrating those decisions on Founders' Day. Their valor and decisiveness are the reasons we are all alive here today. Damn your daughter for her condemnation of our Founders. We're not going to let our society falter because of some stupid girl!"

In less time than it takes to blink, Laurence slides out his sword and lunges for my father. Before my father can grab the hilt of his own sword, Ian slips a knife out from a leg-sheath and slices my father's arm. Two against one, an unspeakable act of unGallantry for such professed adherents to The Lex.

As Jasper tries to make his way through the crowd to rally to my father's defense, Ian and Laurence bear down on my father. He deflects a swipe by Laurence, and he parries Ian's thrust. So paralyzed by shock are the Guards at the pronouncements and the sight of their leaders fighting that the three men continue uninterrupted.

Even with his injury, my father is able to drive Laurence and Ian to the edge of the dais. I breathe a little, thinking that he's about to push them into the throng, when Laurence circles back around my father and places a blade across his neck.

Ian turns toward the people. As he signals Laurence to sever my father's neck, he yells, "This is for New North!"

I will not allow this. I cannot allow this.

I simultaneously unsheathe my sword and run toward the men. Without aforethought or hesitation, as if I'd been born to fight, I slide my blade into Laurence's back, pushing against bone and gristle and organs. Rather than disgust, I feel elation. As if I have excised the rot and decay from this particular garden, so that it can regrow with healthy roots and leaves yearning for the sun.

Perhaps I am the *Angakkuq* after all.

XXXXVII.

Augustus 16
Year 242, A.H.

"Eva . . . Eva . . . Eva . . . Eva."

The people chant their verdict. They will be silent no more.

The Guards finally come to life and take Ian into custody. I reach out to my father to check on his wounds. We embrace, and he whispers, "I'm so sorry, Eva." I don't have to ask what he is sorry for; I know he is apologizing for all of New North.

I look up at the Ring. I want to see if Lukas is appeased, if my words and my actions and my father's deeds and the Aerie's response will stave him off. If I've sacrificed enough of myself to pacify him and the people of the Boundary, before I sacrifice him for killing Eamon.

Placing my hand over my brow for shade, I squint into

the light. Standing alongside the unmistakable outline of Lukas is a sight I thought I'd never see again. A sight I can't even be seeing now. The square shoulders, the angled hair, the jutting chin, and the very particular stance of a singular person in this world. My brother.

No. I shake my head. It's the slap across the face and the fall, or the fact that I just took another human life. Perhaps it's the enormity of this moment. They're causing visions. How else can I can be seeing my dead brother standing on the edge of the Ring?

I dare to look up again, expecting to see Lukas flanked only by his men and not my beloved Eamon. But still Eamon remains at Lukas's side. I even see Lukas lean over to speak to him.

Eamon is real. My brother is alive.

In a tick that seems like eternity, I finally understand everything. Lukas and Eamon needed me to believe in Eamon's death so I could rise up and claim my destiny, a step I could have never taken while Eamon was alive. They knew somehow that Eamon could never have garnered the people's faith, affection, and trust as I have. By claiming my own destiny, they knew that I could help New North claim its own destiny as well.

I should be furious with Lukas and Eamon for deceiving me, for making me suffer and grieve. But I'm not angry at Eamon. My brother is back from the dead; how can I be anything but elated?

And when I think about Lukas—and look over at Jasper, who stands alongside my father on the dais, any anger or confusion I feel is replaced by admiration and appreciation. They have both sacrificed so much for me and for the truth. I've spent so much time debating my feelings for both of them and the right path for myself in New North—Maiden or Boundary, Archon or Lady—but I now understand that I needn't have. I can carve my own path into the snow of New North. Alone if I so choose.

Because together, we've set New North free. Its people are free to break down the walls between Aerie and Boundary and fashion whatever society they agree upon. They are free to select their own roles beyond those to which they are born. And I'm free, too.

I smile up at that spot on the Ring where I see Eamon standing. And even though I know it's impossible, that he's too far away for us to see each other clearly, I swear I see him smile back at me. The time and distance and boundary between us closes, and we are together again as we have always been.

EPILOGUE
November 24
Year 242, A.H.

Little time exists for writing in my journal during these *siniks*. And many, many *siniks* have passed since I've had even a tick to write. The light grows short as winter approaches, and we have much to do. The rebuilding of New North on steady and solid ground requires the whole of our selves, together and as individuals.

The people of New North—*all* the people, Aerie and Boundary alike—did indeed choose freedom. In their quest for a new society built upon a bedrock of freedom without artificial boundaries between people, they chose me as their leader. A Maiden and Archon, young and inexperienced, it's true, but truthful above all. That is all I have, the truth. Perhaps it is enough. But they know I want to earn their leadership, and perhaps in the end, *that* is the quality that is indispensable for this new role, one not borne by the elders of the Aerie. It is truth, but it is also humility in the face of truth.

My *siniks* in the Hall of Archons spent combing through the archives have served me well. Life in the Aerie was not all bad before we learned the truth, not as difficult and inequitable as the lives of those in the days before the flood. The New North did provide for everyone. Nobody went hungry or cold, and nobody will. I wish I could undo the unjust deaths, but we will learn from them as we learn from everything else. I am learning that truth, like food, is best served when needed. With regularity. With even portions.

I am not alone as I lead. Always at my side are my beloved brother Eamon and my trusted advisors Lukas and Jasper. The return of my brother continues to be an unwavering source of delight; I'd gotten so accustomed to his absence that to turn to him for advice never fails to comfort and surprise. It has allowed me to forgive Lukas. For now I know what happened: Lukas and Eamon, and the whole of the Boundary in truth, contrived to feign Eamon's death by using a body laid out in the former Boundary lands for *naasiiviik*, a five-day period of mourning in which a frozen body awaits burial. It was that false body over which my parents wept. They have had a harder time forgiving Lukas—and Eamon, for that matter—but they no longer hold power. And in some ways, like Theo, I think they were relieved to let it go.

So desperate Lukas and his people were to put me in motion! So desperate that they knew the truth I could not see myself: were Eamon alive, I would not have fought. So perhaps they were right. Not that I am the *Angakuuq*. But perhaps they were right to believe that I alone could change New North. Me without Eamon. Apparently Eamon took more convincing, but he came around.

Lukas and Jasper advise me well, too; each helps ensure that the needs and rights of all New Northerners are met. True, they jostle for position beside me as lead counsel. And yes, they still vie for role as future husband, no matter how often I tell them that I intend to enter no Union other than that with the people of New North.

But I rely on both.

Still, leadership is a lonely business. When I feel overwhelmed and no other counsel aids me, I walk through the Passage, as is every New Northerners' right now, and step out onto our land. There amidst the beautiful, blinding whiteness, I might chance upon an *uqalurait*. Lukas's people tell us that these pointed snowdrifts formed by blizzards and resembling a tongue can tell us which direction to go. I will try to follow their guidance.

Although I know too well now to call one text consecrated over any other, if there must be a sacred text for the New Northerners and the people that follow us, perhaps these journals can be a start. Perhaps these may stand as a testament to truth and humility. These are the Books of Eva.

Acknowledgments

THE BOOKS OF EVA never would have emerged from its icy state without the support and encouragement of so many people. I want to start by thanking Laura Dail, who is much, much more than a brilliant, indefatigable agent and a sounding board on all things publishing; she is a true friend. Beginning with my phenomenal editor Dan Ehrenhaft—with whom I shared a mind-meld from the moment we met in the 'burgh—I am so grateful for the amazing Soho Teen team: Soho Teen's tremendous publisher, Bronwen Hruska; my wonderful publicist, Meredith Barnes; as well as the ever-helpful Rachel Kowal and Amara Hoshijo.

Another enormous thanks to all the marvelous educators, librarians, and students who helped make The Books of Eva part of their schools and reading programs—especially my amazing mother-in-law, Catherine Terrell, and her insightful book club members who were so helpful with my Educators' Guide. Other family and friends gave life to The Books of Eva, including my parents; my brothers, sisters, and their spouses; my sister-in-law; Ponny Conomos Jahn; Illana Raia; Mary Zeleny; and our Sewickley network. And a debt of gratitude goes to my beloved Aunt Terry, who started it all.

But the lion's share of the thanks goes to Jim, Jack, and Ben. Without their unwavering love, support, and understanding, I could have never written The Books of Eva. Thank you, boys. For everything.